Spirits of Southeast Alaska

The History & Hauntings of Alaska's Panhandle

By James P. Devereaux

Epicenter Press

Epicenter Press is a regional press publishing nonfiction books about the arts, history, environment, and diverse cultures and lifestyles of Alaska and the Pacific Northwest. For more information, visit www.EpicenterPress.com

www.JamesPDevereaux.com

ISBN: 9781935347675

Library of Congress Control Number: 2016954492

Cover photo Paul Sincic Photo Collection,
courtesy Alaska State Library.
Skagway street view; showing are Pack Train Restaurant, Empire Theatre, Jeff "Soapy" Smith's Parlor (317), New York and Alaska Trading and Mining Co., and others, ca. 1898.

Section photo seen pages viii, 90, 100, 106, 112,
courtesy Library of Congress,
Prints & Photographs Division,
LOT 13947, no. 7,
Reproduction number LC-USZ62-25153

Interior and cover design by Aubrey Anderson

To my dear wife for all of her assistance as my editor, my patient and loving partner and my best friend. To my parents, for making all of this possible.

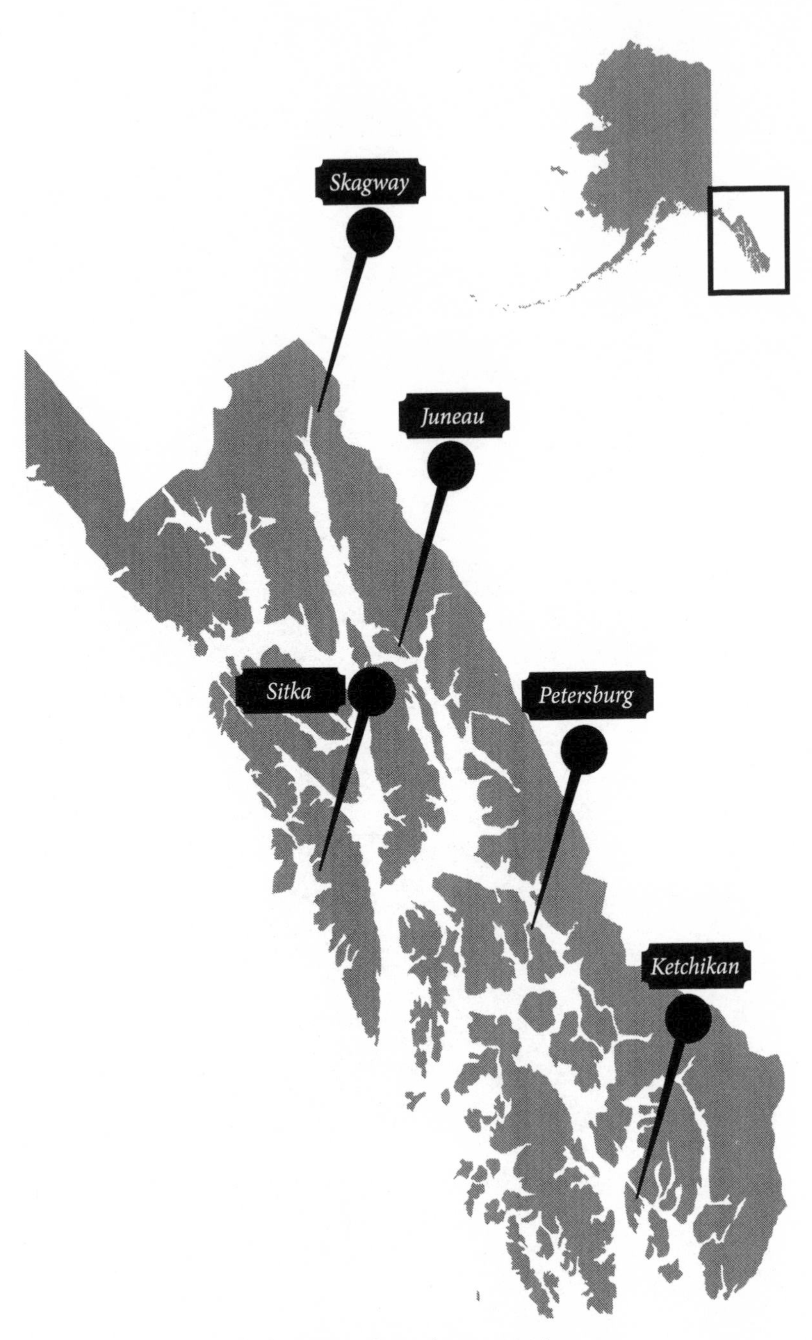

Map of Southeast Alaska

Contents

Foreword

Before the internet and social media; before cell phones, computers, television, radio, and films; before books and writing; before hieroglyphics or cities, there were ghost stories. Just like the smell of bacon beckons memories of breakfast, a ghost story triggers the most primal part of our beings. Darkness, shadows, and spirits walk our dreams and fears. It is when they erupt into our daily lives and intersect with our "reality" that we want to watch and run at the same time. Ghost stories are the folklore of our souls.

As a paranormal researcher and consultant, I have handled hundreds of cases from all over the U.S., and they all start with stories. Stories of the frightening experiences that people have in their homes, cars, in cemeteries, and workplaces. In researching these cases, I strive to discern what is normal—the tapping on the wall coming from tree branches, the shadow in the bedroom at night coming from headlights down the street, the feeling of dizziness and dread coming from the alarm clock near the bed that is leaking large amounts of electromagnetic energy right beside your head. But there are often experiences that remain unexplained. Where more than one person has seen, heard, or felt something, where evidence is captured in audio, photos, or video that corroborates precisely what people have reported. In my field, I strive not to jump into speculation, to stick to what I can document and know from what I don't know. I am a trained historian and museum conservator who often uses science to preserve the artifacts of the past. So I bring that discipline and care to my investigations of spirits.

This book of the Spirits of Southeast Alaska by James Devereaux is a welcome contribution to the literature of ghost stories in the United States. While most collections of ghost stories are rife with unbounded speculation, Devereaux brightens all of these stories with the great foundation of accurate history of the places and people in them. From the Native American villages to the cities and islands where people settled during and after Russian colonization, the Gold Rush, and later the fishing industry, we explore the history and places of Alaska where people lived and died. We encounter specters from princesses, con men, bakers, fishermen, miners, drivers, and more. Often, something strange is seen or heard, sometimes repeatedly, and a place quickly becomes known for this activity. Why?

It's almost impossible to answer without theory and speculation. So, well-told ghost stories are different from investigations because they ultimately need our imaginations. Who is the spirit who was seen? What happened to them? Why do they continue to appear to us? Mr. Devereaux, who is trained in the archaeological sciences, embraces imagination wholeheartedly in answering these questions in the stories in this book. He paints rich portraits of the places and people in Alaska, and the drama of past lives and present apparitions. He helps us visualize the people and events that may have led to these remarkable hauntings in the beautiful towns, islands, mountains, and waters of the inside passage. And that is what makes these stories so enjoyable to read on a dark night when there is a chill in the night.

David Harvey

Paranormal Research and Consultation

www.IDigDeadPeople.weebly.com

Preface

This book was started well before I ever set foot in Alaska, beginning in earnest during the family vacations of my youth. Each summer we took a break from the monotony of city life and traveled somewhere so we could reconnect to our surroundings and to each other.

Sometimes we would spend a week full of sunburn and fun on a sandy beach. Sometimes we spent our time believing in magic again in one of Florida's many amusement parks. Sometimes it was just a quick trip north of our Chicago home to the lake lands of Wisconsin. But the vacations most often taken—and by far my favorites—were the epic American road trips. We would pile into our old minivan, cram the back with camping gear and comfort food, and set off on the open road. As long as I wasn't looking out my brother or sister's window, which my siblings and I strangely agreed was forbidden, I was able to take in sights that instilled in me a life-long curiosity for the world we live in.

The family would tour national parks, paddle down raging rivers, hike through rugged mountains and camp under starry skies. Many a night we would sit around the campfire, bellies loaded with sugar from s'mores, and listen to my father tell ghost story after ghost story. There were a few definite favorites we often heard, such as the story of the Lady of the Lake, who lost her child to a drowning during a terrible storm. She was so overcome by grief that she ended her own life in those waters, only to return on moonlight nights to search in vain for her baby. There was the story of the hunter and his beloved pet monkey, the envy of the hunter's assistant. In a jealous rage one night, the assistant killed the monkey only to have it return from beyond the grave to wreak havoc on the lives of whomever he found. Finally, there was the H.G. Wells's inspired tale of people living below the earth that would creep out from their labyrinths at night seeking food in the form of their distant human cousins. Needless to say, we did not sleep well on these camping trips, as every story told "just happened" to occur upon the ground on which we slept.

Campfire stories like those are perhaps as old as speech itself. A warning to children that not all who enter the woods are safe; that they must remain on their guard lest misfortune befall them. They are meant to entertain, to frighten, and, perhaps, to keep children who are loaded to the gills with sugar from running off into the woods like maniacs.

Not all ghost stories are born of imagination and myth—some have credence. Some have the backing of a trusted eyewitness or even scientific evidence to support them. It was those stories that truly caught my young imagination. A must-do stop on every family trip was a ghost tour. In St. Augustine, Gettysburg, San Antonio, New Orleans, anywhere with a sense of the past, there was always a walking ghost tour that took us through ancient streets and told us tales of real life ghosts, richly woven into the historic tapestry of our surroundings. We were handed electromagnetic frequency detectors that were supposed to signal when ghosts were near and hand held recording devices that could record phantom voices. We were shown photographic evidence of spirits captured at the places we were standing. Though none of our young eyes ever saw anything convincing, and none of the devices I held ever gave forth conclusive evidence, the sincerity of the guides and the facts they presented convinced me their words were true.

These tales were different than those of my father. There was none of the tongue-in-cheek humor, none of the thinly veiled fiction. These were real. Ghosts were real. I began reading everything I could on the subject of paranormal phenomena. Eventually, I got older and my fascination with ghosts faded, but my love of history and adventure burned on. So strong was the pull that I found myself looking for a career that would involve both, which is how I came upon archaeology. For more than a decade now, I have been lucky enough to work throughout the United States, trudging through farm fields, scaling mountains, boating down virgin rivers, all with one goal in mind: to find what those who came before us have left behind and tell their stories—the stories history forgot.

In 2005, this great adventure I set out upon brought me to Alaska for the first time. A lifelong outdoorsman and an avid reader of Jack London and Robert Service, I had always dreamed of seeing the last, great American frontier. It has since become a home, a breeding ground for personal growth and creativity. There I found and fell in love with my beautiful wife, who was kind enough to edit early drafts of this book. I found friendships with truly like-minded people, dedicated to the same principles in life as I. It is where I found myself. There is nothing like the challenges of true wilderness to put one to the test, to boil down all the trivialities surrounding daily life until all that is left is the clean, pure marrow of the soul. Nobody who steps foot on this great land can ever truly walk away. The land is a ghost, forever haunting my subconscious.

Of course, being that it is Alaska, archeology is typically a seasonal occupation, and often a poor paying one at that. To fill the financial gaps I have found myself working jobs that the little boy by the campfire could have never imagined he'd be doing someday. I have built log cabins cut right from the surrounding forest. I have guided people up into the wilderness of the coastal mountains and rafted them back to civilization. I even brought a sleepy, little mountain town its news via the local radio station. It is in this occupation that the idea to write this book was born. One fall, while working for KHNS, the sole radio station of Haines, Skagway and Klukwan, I conceived the idea of having local residents relate ghost stories for a special Halloween broadcast.

The response was overwhelming. Both my email account and my ear at the local saloon became flooded with people eager to tell me the strange things they've seen, the unexplained phenomena that happened to them or a trusted friend. In a short time, I had enough tales to fill an encyclopedia. Unfortunately, archaeology once again called me away from my Alaskan home before the broadcast could come to fruition, but the stories lingered. During the long, lonely nights I spent protecting America's cultural resources during the Deepwater Horizon oil spill in the Gulf of Mexico, I began writing the stories, distilling them into the spirit of Southeast Alaska's paranormal phenomena.

In this volume, I have tried to include not only the most viable of ghost stories, but also included stories that help tell, in the most general of terms, the rich history of the land many of you are imagining as you read these tales. It is important to me that the reader understands the historical background of these ghost stories. Without such information these tales are merely campfire s'mores, delicious but without any sustaining qualities. Alaska is the last place on earth I want you to go running off into the woods like a maniac on a sugar high. Enjoy this labor of love and keep your senses heightened as you embark on a grand adventure into the historical hauntings of the Last Frontier.

The Baranof Castle in Sitka, Alaska, ca. 1900-1910.
William A. Langille Photo Collection,
courtesy Alaska State Library.

The Ghosts of Indian River and Castle Hill, and the Princess of Baranof Castle

Castle Hill and the Indian River are sites of ancient Tlingit villages and fortifications, eventually becoming the capital of Russian America and the site where Russia signed over Alaska to the United States. This landscape has seen numerous instances of bloodshed and horror. Today, mysterious wailing, drumbeats, and a mournful female spirit are said to regularly occur over the hollowed historical ground.

All evidence available today suggests that the first white men to set foot on Alaskan soil came from Russia. In 1648, the explorer Semyon Dezhnev was mapping out the eastern extremes of Siberia when, as legend tells, several ships in his fleet were caught in a mighty gale. The winds swept them to the east, across the narrow waters of what is today known as the Bering Sea and onto the Alaskan coast. These men supposedly established a settlement, though no evidence of such a place has yet been found. What is known is that Dezhnev's expedition and rumors of a land connection to North America near Kamchatka inspired Tsar Peter I to mount a second expedition in 1725, this one under the command of a much more familiar name, Vitus Bering.

Bering's three-year expedition proved that Russia and North America were separated by a narrow sea, which was eventually named after the explorer himself. He returned home a hero and rose immediately in the ranks of Russian aristocracy. He amassed wealth and influence and was chosen to lead a second expedition into North America. Following a series of delays and political maneuvering, the Second Kamchatka expedition was finally launched in 1741. Only 46 of the original 77 men survived the voyage, but word of the rich lands to the east spread like wildfire. Of particular interest to the Russian people were the tales of an endless supply of valuable fur seal and sea otter, prized for their use in fashionable headwear and clothing in European society. Almost overnight, droves of Siberian fur traders and missionaries flocked into this unknown land. The first great push to control the valuable resources of the Alaskan territory was on.

Before long, hunting and trading posts extended into the landscape well beyond the area Bering first surveyed. Many of the settlers in these outposts consisted of indigenous peoples of Eastern Russia and Siberia, most of whom were genetically similar to the people already living in the area. In spite of similar appearance and culture, indigenous Siberians and their more ethnically European Russian counterparts did not treat the Alaska Natives well. Rapidly increasing competition for furs in the new land quickly led to indifference and brutality toward those who had occupied the land for millennia. Many Aleut people were reduced to a state of slavery, forced to hunt the fur-bearing mammals that made their masters rich. The atrocities committed in the pursuit of conquest and wealth are too numerous to mention and far scarier than any ghostly tale.

In 1790, the newly organized Russian-American Company established a settlement on the Northeastern side of Kodiak Island. The company was led by the territorial governor of Alaska, Alexander Andrevevich Baranof. Before long, this 15-year-old runaway turned successful trader would become known as the "Lord of Alaska." A bright and vigorous man, his sphere of influence would soon spread deep into the inside passage and beyond. He was a man of great duality. Today he is remembered in Russia as a generous benefactor to Alaska's native inhabitants and the bringer of education and missionary settlements into the territory. Not all remember Baranof fondly in Southeast Alaska today. Despite his good deeds, many remember a brutal and effective conqueror who destroyed any opposition to Russian hegemony. Even today, in the shadow of his greatest military victory, his named is forever attached by some to a ruthless history etched into the bloodied granite of a lonely hill in Sitka.

By 1795, Baranof had become concerned with the ever increasing numbers of British, European, and American Fur traders encroaching on Russian territories near today's Pacific Northwest and British Columbia. Something had to be done to protect Russian interests. By the end of 1795, Baranof had met with a band of Tlingit near present day Sitka. He paid them for exclusive access to fur trading within the region. What he failed to realize, however, was Tlingit bands throughout Southeast Alaska operated more like city-states than a unified people. In order to seek such privileges the Russians needed to negotiate with all clans and villages within the Tlingit landscape.

Within the next several years, Baranof decided to move his base of company operations, now known as the Russian-American Company, from Kodiak Island to an area in Sitka Sound that was ideal for habitation. The forests were mighty Sitka spruce and western hemlock, strong yet flexible trees good for construction of ships and buildings. Food was also seemingly abundant. The rivers teemed with salmon and fur-bearing sea mammals were present in large numbers. One sight in particular had caught Baranof's attention in the 1795 expedition: a large granite outcropping, rising just above the water and looming over the bay. It was a veritable Gibraltar of the new world, a perfect site for a fortification and a statement to all parties daring to challenge Russian supremacy in this rich land. Unfortunately for his plans, the hill was already occupied by a Tlingit fort and encampment called Noow Tlein, or Big Fort. Baranof decided upon a second spot in what is known today as Starrigavan Bay or Old Harbor, about seven miles north of Big Fort. There Baranof established a stockade supported settlement, complete with barracks, a blacksmith shop, livestock barns, various other necessary structures and a wilderness estate for Baranof himself.

The peace between the Russians and the Tlingit was short lived. A pattern of brutal treatment by the Russians and competition for resources soon boiled over. On June 20, 1802, the settlement was attacked by a Tlingit army in full battle regalia from nearby Indian Creek on Sitka Island. To the Russians surprise, they were armed not only with their customary spears and clubs, but also with a large cache of modern guns. These guns were most likely acquired through trade with European and American trading vessels that regularly visited the Inside Passage. The battle resulted in a catastrophic loss for the Russian colony. Almost every man within the walls of the stockade was massacred. Twenty Russian and 130 Aleut bodies were strewn about the grounds, mutilated and left to rot. The poor women and children who survived the massacre were subsequently enslaved and brought back as war trophies to the Big Fort hill and the Indian River Village. Perhaps it is the lonely spirit of one of these poor women—a captive who witnessed the death of her loved ones and everything she held dear—who haunts the hill to this very day.

Baranof was infuriated by the loss. By 1804, he had amassed

an army and set sail for Sitka with the Russian warship *Neva* accompanying for artillery support. What they found upon their arrival was a village ready for a fight. The Tlingit had constructed another fort less than a mile from Big Fort made of more than 1,000 Sitka Spruce trees. Called Shís'gi Noow or the "Fort of the Young Saplings," it was located adjacent to a long and wide gravel bar that extended so far out into the bay that any ship would have a hard time bringing their guns in close enough to fire at the Natives' forts. The plan for the Tlingit was to initially begin fighting with the Russians at Big Fort and gauge their enemy's strength. Once the number of Russians was better established, the Tlingit plan was to either head to the Fort of the Young Saplings, or retreat over the mountains to another village site.

Initial demands by the Russians were for the immediate surrender of Big Fort on the hill, which were rejected. On September 29, the Russians spotted a canoe full of elders returning with a large supply of gunpowder and immediately began firing. The canoe, its occupants, and the gunpowder were blown to smithereens. Such a loss of noblemen and leaders was devastating to the Tlingit. Wails of mourning mixed with cries of rage echoed along the harbor.

On October 1, the warship *Neva* was towed into close range of the Indian River Fort, which Tlingit forces now occupied. The shelling began, and Baranof with more than five hundred men, led an assault on the Fort of the Young Saplings. It was quickly a grudge match of brutal hand-to-hand combat. The day appeared nearly lost for the Tlingit, until a planned second wave of warriors from the woods crushed the Russians with a classic pincer movement. Baranof himself was seriously wounded in the assault, and the Russians were forced to hastily retreat.

A badly wounded Baranof ordered his ships to begin a steady bombardment of the fortifications. Throughout the day, the cannonade continued and by nightfall a call for surrender was issued. The Tlingit scoffed at the idea but, realizing that they could never contend with the cannon fire from the ships, began a preplanned withdrawal from the area.

Women and able-bodied children slipped out first, bound for a northern bay where they would construct a new village. Upon landing ashore, the Russians were horrified to find that all of the infants and dogs within the Tlingit fortresses were killed that night. The Tlingit were frightened that a safe retreat would be foiled due to the wailing of the babes and the howling of the dogs, so all were summarily clubbed to death. It is not known how many infants were lost that night, but the number of warriors within the fort was estimated to be around eight hundred. Scores of children were killed to ensure the survival of the people as a whole. Having to make such a terrible choice is almost unbearable in itself.

For two more days the unrelenting bombardment of the forts continued, and for two more days, negotiations for a truce and the secret escape of hundreds of Tlingit tribal members continued. Finally, mercifully, the Russians heard echoing over the placid water of Sitka Harbor, a lone and final war song from Big Fort. This ancestral fortification, occupied since at least 1,000 AD by Native peoples of Alaska, was gone from their grasp. The pounding of the drum and wailing cries of despair at its conclusion told the tale that the Russians had succeeded. The bay and the Strait of Gibraltar to the west that guarded her was theirs. The remaining Tlingit warriors slipped into the dark forest under cover of night, escaping to the northern extreme of the island, joining what remained of their shattered families.

After several more days of cautious observation, the Russians made landfall and discovered the horrific extremes the Tlingit had taken to ensure their safe escape. The diary of a Russian Captain by the name of Lisianski speaks well to the feeling of the men upon observing the brutal tactics employed for survival:

> Having come ashore, I observed the most barbaric sight that could bring even the most hardened heart

> to tremble and recoil. Assuming that we could trace them in the woods by the voices of infants and dogs, the Sitkans put them all to death… the entire set of circumstances led us to conclude that the fortress had contained no less than 800 persons of male gender.

Disgusted and battle weary, the Russians occupied their prized hilltop fortification and destroyed the fort at Indian Creek, ensuring that it could never again be used by the Sitka Tlingit.

The Russians erased the Native presence in what they called New Archangel. The hill known as Noow Tlein was renamed after Baranof. A sizable fort was built on ancestral Tlingit lands atop the charred ruins and dead bodies. The structure was impressive in scope and size. Space for thirty-two cannons allowed for accurate artillery fire over the bay and passage to the west. There was a high wooden palisade surrounding it, several logs thick. Three enclosed watchtowers for lookouts and sharpshooters afforded a commanding view of the surrounding countryside. By 1805, at least eight buildings were constructed within the walls. The sixty-foot high hill and its mighty fortifications secured Russia's dominance in the region, but it was not maintained without difficulty. Occasional skirmishes and raids continued from the Tlingit, though they never mounted a successful sacking of a settlement on Sitka Island.

By 1838, the fortification on the hill had evolved into a veritable palace on the Russian frontier. It served as the capital and governmental seat of Russian America as well as the home for the governor of the territory. In 1818, Russian America's famed Governor Baranof had retired, never to see this final manifestation of his sought after fortress on the hill. It is a testament to his fame, rather than his actual deeds, that the castle bears his name. Rather than the opulent, stone, old-world palace that usually accompanies the word "castle," Baranof's Castle was instead a three story wooden framed structure. Built of cedar planking with a wooden cupola on top, it was surrounded by a palisade wall.

Though the exterior was impressive, it was certainly not up to snuff with contemporary structures in existence at the time. The interior of the structure, however, was lavish for its day. It boasted brass chandeliers, large meeting halls, governmental offices and sleeping quarters for the governor, military officers, and their families, and honored guests. A constant stream of diplomats, visiting dignitaries, aristocratic vacationers and wealthy traders stayed within its walls during the golden age of Russian Sitka. While European and American trading companies continued to exert further and further influence on the Inside Passage, the Russian Empire eagerly exploited the remaining power it held in the region from this opulent seat upon the rock. It is during this particular time period that the ghost or ghosts associated with what is now named Castle Hill appear to have originated. It is here that the ghostly history of Castle Hill begins.

There are few ghost stories in Southeast Alaska, and North America for that matter, that have enjoyed the longevity and the exaggerations than that the ghost of the Lady in Black of Baranof's Castle has enjoyed. In fact, in researching the story I found several versions in print that are so outlandish and easily disprovable through simple archival research that they are not even worth telling. What is worth telling, however, are the reports that were written down consistently, all telling of a very similar series of phenomena in similar parts of the hilltop castle.

The traditional legend says that within the walls of Baranof's Castle walks the ghost of a long dead, beautiful Russian princess or member of the aristocracy. The first recording of this tale of sorrow and betrayal comes to us from the August 22nd, 1883 edition of *The New York Times*. Supposedly, at the hour of midnight, the shadowy figure of a woman dressed all in black emerges out of the dark, abandoned ballroom and walks the halls mourning an unknown loss.

> She wears long, trailing black robes, and her forehead, neck and wrists are flashing with diamonds. She wrings

> her beautiful, white hands and wanders, with sorrowful mien, from room to room, and leaves a faint perfume as of wild roses where she passes.

The article states that numerous American naval officers and sailors had tried to spend the night alone in the castle, but none had done it successfully, always fleeing for safety from the ghostly happenings in the castle before the sunrise the following day.

In the most popular form of the legend, this poor grief-stricken spirit was the daughter or niece of one of the territorial governors, though the possibility of the spirit being a daughter of a governor is highly unlikely. No territorial governor is known to have had a female child survive into adulthood. Nevertheless, the legend goes, this noblewoman was renowned both in her native homeland and in her new life in Sitka for her beauty and grace. Never before had this frontier outpost encountered such a creature, men both noble and common immediately fell in love with her.

Despite an endless series of suitors the princess remained virtuous and pure, her heart kept close and patient. Finally, during a grand ball held at the castle, the princess' eyes met with a handsome young prince who was serving aboard one of the trading vessels frequenting the harbor. Their mutual attraction soon blossomed into a deep and profound love. They would frequently sneak off to the mouth of Indian Creek to declare their undying affection for one another. Unfortunately, another much older and nefarious prince would soon arrive in Sitka and seek to destroy their blossoming romance.

He was a brutal and sinful man. According to legend, he lost numerous fortunes in his life through vice, crime and evil deeds. He came to Sitka seeking his fourth fortune at the reluctant invitation of the governor, who he knew from Russia. Unfortunately, during that time, the evil prince discovered the governor was involved in an unsuccessful revolutionary plot, a treasonous act punishable by death. Such a crime, if found out, was surely capable of ruining the governor's life, as well as the life of his entire family. The prince knew this, and used it to his advantage time and time again. Upon his arrival, he was introduced to the princess and was immediately taken by her beauty. He knew her as a girl in Russia, and had always harbored a desire for her. Before long, the prince told the governor he wanted to marry the princess. The governor was well aware that she loved another, but he approved heartily of the match because he had no a choice. The refusal of the evil prince's request would be certain death or banishment to him and his entire family.

The governor called upon the princess the next day, and told her of her fate. The young woman was devastated and instantly refused the arrangement. In response, the governor banned her young lover forever from the castle on the hill and endeavored to remove him from Russian America altogether. He was not successful in his efforts to alienate the young prince. The love between the two was so profound that nothing could stop it. They continued to meet in secret at their spot along the banks of the Indian River, just outside of the shadows of the castle. One day, the evil prince followed the pair to the river and reported the tryst to the governor, threatening exposure if the lovers were not parted at once. The governor acted quickly and decisively.

The next morning, he announced that an expedition was headed southward, leaving that very day, in order to ascertain the position of enemy trading posts along the frontier. The young prince was selected as one of the officers of the reconnaissance vessel. Once aboard the vessel, the trap was sprung. The prince was locked below deck, unable to escape and separated indefinitely from his love. The princess, unaware that her lover was being held against his will, waited patiently as days turned into weeks and weeks turned into months. She feared the worst but could not bring herself to accept that he was gone. Still, in spite of the possibility of her lover's death, she refused to marry the evil prince. Finally, after several months with no sign of his return, she agreed to marry the evil prince on the condition that they wait until March 18th, the birthday of the governor. Every night, until the night before the wedding, the princess would light a lantern and climb up to the cupola. She scanned the seas to the south, desperately looking for any sign of the vessel that carried all the love and hope she had in the world.

Alas, no sign came. On March 18th, clad in a flowing silk dress and adorned in diamonds, the princess was wed to the evil prince in St. Michael's Cathedral. Afterward, a lavish celebration was held at the castle. Fine wines and champagne were toasted to the future of the couple. Food which was seldom seen on the Russian frontier was enjoyed. Merriment and laughter filled the halls and hearts, except one heart. The princess, ashen with despair, spoke barely a word, and seemed at death's door from sorrow. Suddenly, a boom from the southernmost watchtower resounded through the castle, announcing the arrival of a friendly vessel. Feigning illness, the princess excused herself from the festivities and ran to the cupola. There, mooring into the harbor, was the ship of her love. She ran to the spot of their lover's trysts waiting for his arrival.

Out of the darkness, the young man approached, and they locked in a passionate embrace. In the distance, the enraged calls of her new husband echoed throughout the valley. A line of men with torches appeared from the castle walls, hurriedly heading in the direction of the well-known rendezvous spot. Trapped on the island, with no possibility of escape, facing certain death for their infidelity, the young couple decided that it was better to die together on the banks of the river where they fell in love than separately at the gallows. With one last kiss, they unsheathed hidden blades, pierced their hearts and fell dead on the banks of the Indian River. As they held one another, their blood mixed together for all eternity and washed out to sea. When the men arrived, the heartbroken governor collapsed in sorrow, cursing the mistakes of his youth and the tragedy he caused. He buried them, still locked in their embrace, at the banks of the river they lived and died on.

Following her death, stories have been reported of her spirit walking the halls of Baranof's Castle. She is sometimes described as wearing blue or black flowing garments, most likely her wedding dress. Interestingly, traditional Russian wedding attire of the time was white, so possibly the color is a reflection of her eternal anguish and sorrow. In some of the accounts, she holds a single candle or lantern in her hand, and she seems to be searching for something that isn't there. Often, the spirit was seen in the cupola of the Castle, her eyes fixed out on the horizon to the south, forever searching for her lover. Many witnesses reported seeing her eyes fill with tears and noticed a flowing wound on her breast. Just before disappearing, she is said to gaze up at whoever had spied her and lets out a bloodcurdling, anguished cry before disappearing. Is this a cry of pain at the self-inflicted wound? Or is it derived from the anguish she felt at the separation of her lover?

Perhaps the ghost that haunts the grounds is not this legendary princess at all. Perhaps it is instead the ghost of one of the women captured by the Tlingit in the destruction of Old Sitka in 1799. These poor unfortunates, forced to witness the brutal deaths of their husbands and families during the Battle of Old Sitka only to be doomed to a life of brutal servitude in a foreign land could certainly be haunting this place. Perhaps the ghostly hauntings are instead the ghosts of the Tlingit warriors themselves, forever reliving the loss of their ancestral lands and the murder of their children by their own hands. To this day, phantom wails and cries that seem to have no source are heard at night near the old fortification. Drum beats and war songs are sometimes heard floating along the breeze. Could these sounds be the ghosts of those killed in the Battle of Sitka, forever crying out their final triumphant war song?

It is also interesting to note that in 1867 Castle hill became the site of Russia's sale of her Alaskan territory to the United States. Could it be that these mournful cries are the ghost of

Baranof himself? This man of singular drive and accomplishment would certainly be devastated to see the empire he built sold off for pennies? Though long dead by the time of Seward's Folly—the purchase of Alaska from Russia in 1867—perhaps his lingering spirit remains in the seat of his empire. No matter the source of these hauntings, the sorrows spilled out onto this small space have certainly left their mark. The memory of the terrible losses and evil deeds remain in the soil to this day.

What does not remain is Baranof Castle itself. On the eve of March 18, 1894, the anniversary of the death of the Princess, a fire broke out in the dry, ancient wooden structure. Abandoned since the sale of Russian America to the United States, the property started being restored in 1893. The rooms where the fire began were converted into the Sitka District Court, but some say that it was once the ballroom where the princess first set eyes upon her handsome prince. The cause of this fire remains unknown. The only evidence of the structure today is a memorial plaque and a few interpretive signs at the Baranof Castle State Historic Site.

The old Baranof Castle, engulfed in flames.
Michael Z. Vinokouroff Photo Collection, courtesy Alaska State Library.

Facade of Mascot Saloon, 1898, Broadway Avenue, City of Skagway, Alaska.

Photo courtesy Library of Congress, Prints & Photographs Division, HABS, Reproduction number HABS AK,18-SKAG,1--15.

Ghosts of the Mascot Saloon

The Mascot Saloon has numerous reports of poltergeist activity and ghostly voices that were documented by several members of the National Park Service as well as cruise ship visitors. The bathrooms and the upstairs offices, particularly the archaeological storage area, have long been believed to contain energies from beyond the grave.

The Mascot Saloon is one of the few drinking establishments in town remaining similar in appearance to those built in the tumultuous first days of Skagway's existence as the gateway to the Klondike. Located on the corner of 3rd Avenue and Broadway Street, the Mascot is one of the few structures within Skagway's historic district that has never been relocated.

The saloon is considered to be the oldest drinking establishment operated by the same owner within gold rush era Skagway. The land on which it sits was once part of the 160-acre Moore Homestead and was staked after the miners land grab of Moore's property by a J.A. Doc Cleveland. Cleveland was an early arrival to the valley and by June of 1897 was operating as a packer up the White Pass Trail, transporting goods and food when hired by miners. Respecting Moore's original 160-acre homestead claim, Cleveland did not officially assume ownership of the territory where he operated until September of 1897. At that time, the lots sat just above the high tide line and were subject to periodic flooding.

It's very possible that some of the reported paranormal activity on the property is a result of its use by Cleveland prior to the construction of the saloon. The harsh condition of life on the fringes of the Northern Lynn Canal is often brutal. A fine, silty glacial muck would be mixed with the refuse of the pack animals and invariably cling to everything it touched. Every step in such misery would be a challenge. Between grueling and often fatal trips up the Dead Horse Trail, the pack animals would be put into pens that were little more than mud troughs. On especially rainy days or during high tides they found themselves fighting with the wet ground to keep from sinking up to their bellies. The tree-bare plain was exposed to brutal winds and weather funneled up the canal, and southern storm systems could bring days-constant storms.

The advantage of an inhospitable waterfront location was it allowed Cleveland's packing operation to be one of the first businesses miners would see when reaching Skagway. A newly arrived "Cheechako"—a person new to the mining districts of Alaska or northwestern Canada—with his grubstake sinking in muck next to an ever rising tide, was an easy sell in the merits of having a ready and waiting wagon team take his goods to dry land. But it was not prospectors' supplies that Cleveland became known for hauling, it was something far more macabre—something that perhaps explains the hauntings at the Mascot.

On August 11, 1897 an unfortunate soul named Dwight B. Fowler was crossing the Skagway River with a full pack of goods. As was far too often the case on the White Pass, Fowler's ambitions exceeded his abilities. The sheer force of the rushing Skagway

River on his 100-plus pound pack proved too much, and he found himself swept downstream. Even without the weight of a pack, the Skagway River can be fatal to the unwary traveler. The glacially fed water is only a few degrees above freezing at its warmest and is capable of inducing hypothermia within minutes. It's also full of fine silt capable of filling pockets and boots in seconds. Trees and other debris litter the channels and, unfortunately, the power of the river against the immobile branches forces the victim under the water and into the tangles of other limbs. Such was the case this day, and the first official casualty of the Skagway River was recorded.

After fishing Fowler's body out of the river, a hastily assembled committee decided Cleveland was to bring the remains back to his packing operation in Skagway. To the dismay of the miners, Cleveland would not perform the deed unless he received his customary $10 packing fee. The miners refused to pay, so Cleveland simply fished through the pockets of the dead man until he procured his fee. He continued on his way down the slopes to his waterfront lots, where Fowler's mortal remains were stored in the exposed and swampy lot. Where he was eventually interred is lost to history, though the tidelands of Alaska have been known to swallow cars in a single event. Could the brutality of life and death on the tidelands and man's indifference to fellow man have provoked Fowler's spirit?

Regardless of his final resting place, the soul of Dwight B. Fowler could very well be the source of reported ghostly activity in the Mascot Saloon. Over the years, visitors and employees have seen the Mascot's first-floor bathroom faucets turn on and off by themselves and have felt icy, cold spots pass through the premises. There are reports of the men's bathroom hand dryers turning on when no one is nearby. Park Service employees have also reported doors on the first floor locking and unlocking by themselves without anyone with keys near the building. This activity occurs behind the structure in which the original Mascot was housed, where a storage shed stood in photographs dating to that time.

Could this area be the last resting place of the drowned and mistreated Fowler? Are the icy waters and filthy conditions he faced in life and early death forever played out here with water faucets in bathrooms?

It is uncertain if anything remains of Fowler within the saloon itself. What is certain is that from the beginning, the Mascot property was witness to the harsh realities of life and death in the Last Frontier. The respite and enjoyment the saloon provided seems to have left an impression upon the grounds as much as the sorrow. In 1974, the building was acquired by the National Park Service and the saloon was restored to its gold rush appearance. On numerous occasions since, members of the National Park Service janitorial staff working after hours have reported the clinking of glasses and the raucous laughter of men in the bar room. One even reported the unmistakable odor of cigar smoke filling her nostrils well after the doors leading to busy Broadway Street were locked.

A separate haunting has been observed in the second floor that may have little to do with the history of the structure, but rather a tale far more tragic. The area has known many uses since the initial construction of the structure in March of 1898. First used as office space, it eventually served as lavish wine parlor and was converted to apartments used by long-lasting saloon proprietor Albert Reinert from 1899 through 1918.

The upstairs is now used as the park's archaeological offices and artifact storage area. It is in this storage area, a mysterious large room accessible to few within the park staff, where this next haunting is rooted. You see, the room houses many lost and lonely possessions of the poor souls who perished in the Palm Sunday Avalanche of 1898.

In the spring during the Klondike Gold Rush, the Chilkoot

Trail was a mess of strenuous chaos. Famed writer and naturalist John Muir visited the area in 1899 and described the scene as "a nest of ants taken into a strange country and stirred up by a stick." The lust for gold conquered men's minds, and they often abandoned safety and reason to stay ahead of fellow miners on the long march to riches. Such was the abandonment that took many of the men who marched goods up Long Hill above Sheep Camp on April 3, 1898.

Winter's grip was finally loosening in lower elevations, though snow continued to pound the mountaintops. In the days preceding Palm Sunday, a warm, southerly wind blew up the valley causing the snowpack to become extremely unstable. The Native Alaskan packers and experienced "sourdoughs"—an experienced prospector in the western U.S. or Canada, named for the pouches of sourdough starter they carried to make bread on the go—knew to stay off the trail because of avalanche danger, but hundreds of men continued to carry their goods through the narrow valley to the Scales encampment—a small bowl just below the final 1,000-foot near-vertical climb to the summit.

The day prior to Palm Sunday a number of smaller avalanches struck the trail, killing several miners. When reports of the calamities made it to the Scales, survival instinct finally took over the gold hungry crowd, and those in transit decided to evacuate immediately.

The first to head back were a group of Chilkoot Railroad and Transportation Company construction workers. While making a path those behind could follow, they came upon a blinding snowstorm, became disoriented and wandered off the main trail into a narrow ravine where a roaring wave of snow and debris buried them. Trekking behind the construction workers, and completely unaware of the disaster ahead, were more than two hundred miners and pack animals. In order to stay together, the group held onto a large rope. The workers trail, which appeared to be a well-trodden guide to the salvation of Sheep Camp, turned out to be a road to doom. Once in the narrow canyon, the vibrations from the group's footsteps triggered another massive avalanche. The miners in the front of the rope line were buried under fifty feet of snow. Runners were sent and warning shots were fired off, and about 1,000 men from Sheep Camp hurried up the trail to help in the rescue effort. Reports are conflicting as to how many men perished in the avalanches of Palm Sunday, but figures range from about forty to seventy with some estimates as high as 120.

Not all of the men had the luxury of a quick death. Many spent hours slowly suffocating under the snow—their prayers and whispers locked in ice. Those who were not shipped home for burial were laid to rest in the Slide Cemetery outside of Dyea. What goods they had stayed where they lay, marking forever the scene of so many deaths with a simple memorial of picks and shovels, pans and shoes.

In 1968, the State of Alaska completed an eight-year project recreating the Chilkoot as a recreational trail. When the National Park Service resurveyed the trail in the 1970s, it was discovered that about eighty percent of Chilkoot Trail artifacts had disappeared or were in an advanced stage of decomposition. Because of this alarming trend, and in hopes of preserving the physical memories of the trail for future generations, the NPS embarked on several ambitious archaeological surveys, which in 1979 led archaeologists to the Palm Sunday Avalanche site.

Because the area was away from the present-day Chilkoot Trail, it had escaped the bulk of the looting that destroyed the visual remnants of much of the ghost towns and pathways. It was as if the area had been consciously left alone by later miners. Much of what was left—personal keepsakes, mining equipment or long since spoiled food containers—was brought down from the mountains. Following analysis of the artifacts, they were stored in the second floor of the Mascot Saloon. It appears the artifacts did not come alone.

In the summer of 2009, park archaeologist Shawn Jones went to his second floor office after work to catch up on unfinished business. By day, the Mascot Saloon serves as a major tourist attraction. But at night, when the crowds are gone and the midnight sun is slipping behind the mountains, an eerie quiet fills the halls.

On this July night, Jones unlocked the door leading to the upstairs offices and was startled at the sound of large pieces of crashing metal coming from the second floor. Racing up the stairs fearing a collapse of the building, Jones was shocked to find nothing wrong or out of place. He decided the noise came from the storage area next to his office, but there was no response to his knock save what he assumed were the calm steady footsteps of the quiet curator, who often worked with headphones blaring and oblivious to those around her. Jones figured she must have dropped something while taking annual inventory and went about his work.

As the night wore on, there was more crashing followed by the soft footsteps. Just as he was about to leave, the office door opened and in walked the curator he thought was already in the building. She had come to check on a few things in the storage area before retiring for the evening.

Upon opening the locked door, to which only three people in the park have the key, they found nothing out of order. Every artifact was in its place, every box sat on the shelf where it belonged. Nothing in the realm of the physical had made those horrible crashing noises, and nothing walked through the room but the past.

Could the traumatic events of April 3 be replaying through the possessions of the deceased now housed in the Mascot?

Jones's tale is one of many unnatural events park archaeologists and curators have reported. One spoke of phantom knocks that seemed to begin from the storage area and then continue faintly around the office. Could this be a lost spirit forever desperately knocking, seeking freedom from the crushing snows? It is not known where or why such activity originates, but it is known that whatever remains there appears to have a playful side as well. Desk chairs are often raised to their maximum height, making it impossible to sit. Desk items that disappear for days at a time are returned to the very spot they were last seen.

The ghostly footsteps continue to occasionally walk the storage facility, perhaps grateful to feel the solid earth beneath their feet, instead of the endless snows.

Portside view of the Princess Sophia, smoke streaming from stack.

Winter and Pond. Photo Collection,
courtesy Alaska State Library.

The Ghost of the Princess Sophia

Stories of ghostly lights along the Vanderbilt Reef, music that has no origin, and the wails and cries of unseen ship's passengers abound at the sight of the Inside Passage's greatest maritime tragedy.

The windswept fjords of the Inside Passage appear to the newly arrived Cheechako as a largely untamed wilderness. With the exception of the occasional harbor town or fishing boat, travelers are presented with a grand frontier; a place devoid of the tracks of mankind and the influence of civilization. Little do most realize they are surrounded by remnants of human history spanning over 10,000 years. Where now there is a cruise ship or a freight barge cutting through the fjords, there once was a proud parade of long canoes returning from a successful hunt. Where now there is a lone island in the channel, there was once an emergency shelter alee of one of the great and terrible storms that rise on the water. These stories will likely remain untold, but there is one period of time everyone can agree influenced Alaska's path greatly.

When word of the Klondike River's gold-rich claims reached a recession-weary United States in the summer of 1897, a powder keg of enthusiasm was set off. Soon, much of the world turned its attention to the northern frontier. Hundreds of thousands of souls scrambled as fast as they could by any means necessary to get to the boomtown of Dawson City and her many gold-laden streambeds. Particularly impacted by gold fever were the North American towns along the Pacific Coast. The first announcement that millionaire miners were headed home to the United States on the vessels *Excelsior* in San Francisco and the *Portland* in Seattle set the West Coast ablaze. So frenzied was the fever pitch toward the North that even Seattle Mayor William D. Wood resigned his position and headed to the Yukon. Within a matter of days every vessel that could float—and some that could not—were headed north through the treacherous Inside Passage.

The great Klondike Gold Rush, although it was in Canada, was an undeniably shining, albeit brief, moment in time for coastal Southeast Alaska. By 1903, less than a decade after the initial gold strike, heavy equipment was brought into the claims surrounding Dawson. Corporations quickly bought out small time operations and before long, the days of independent placer mining on the Klondike River were largely over. Miners short on luck quickly abandoned the boomtowns of the Klondike in droves, and once-thriving communities became blustery outposts in the wilderness. The town of Dyea at the head of the Chilkoot Trail, which once claimed 8,000 residents, had become ghost town with only a handful of occupants by 1900. For years it served as a farm, but the buildings and streets soon disappeared into the rivers and forests. Though also in decline, some other towns had managed to weather the storm.

Due to its being an interior entry point via the White Pass, at its height Skagway boasted a population of as many as 10,000 people. After the gold rush, Skagway turned into a town of around 1,000. She survived into the twentieth century because of her narrow gauge railroad. Constructed over the White Pass by 1899, the railroad to Whitehorse served as the primary route for goods, services and people entering the now booming interior of the Yukon from the southern Pacific. From the Whitehorse railroad depot, riverboats would ferry passengers and goods down the Yukon River to Dawson and towns beyond. During the overall decline of commerce in the Klondike, Skagway and her railroad had come to depend on those traveling to and from the interior for business, and would deeply feel the pain of the greatest maritime disaster in the Inside Passage. However, there was another once mighty town that would suffer far more loss.

Dawson City was the very heart of the Gold Rush. Opulent by any standards, during her heyday almost anything could happen for a price. Champagne and caviar, women and wine, drugs and dirges were available for the lucky few who could afford the astronomical fees. But fortune is fickle and before long the newer strikes and other dreams had led the mining community away. Mining was still done by large-scale operations for a time, but by 1918, the city, which once boasted a population of more than 30,000, had declined to a town of about 2,000. Dawson's remaining residents still slept a stone's throw away from the fabled gold fields, but every year the number of men and women employed in the mining profession shrank.

By 1918, rather than mining, it was the shipping and transportation industry that brought food to the table in Dawson City. Residents put down their picks and shovels and began working paddle wheelers to facilitate the growth of boomtowns further downstream when the Yukon River was ice-free. Other residents bought and sold goods, which came via rail from Skagway to Whitehorse and were shipped up and down the river. Those involved in these trades were seasonal employees, often owning homes in Pacific Northwestern seaports. Just like today, much of the Klondike's population spent the summer toiling in the midnight sun and in the fall sought warmer climates and the comforts of civilization available in the southlands. The only way out that was practical was the same way most got in to begin with—a riverboat to the rapids of Whitehorse, an overland trip via the White Pass & Yukon Railroad and a long steamship ride south.

It was a chilly October 23rd, 1918 and well past the final blooms of the fireweed when the *Princess Sophia* pulled out of Skagway's harbor for the last time. She was full to capacity with a varied group made up of frontiersmen, civic figureheads, miners, boat crews, railroaders, families and soldiers headed off to the first great world war. Though there may have been many more, a total of 353 passengers and crew, including fifty women and children, were officially logged in for travel to Seattle and ports in between. The ship was the last vessel leaving the Upper Lynn Canal for the season and many were desperate to get out. Little did they realize at the time how well they would soon know the meaning of desperation.

The *SS Princess Sophia* was a steel-hulled vessel the Canadian Pacific Railway began operating in 1911. One of four Princess series coastal passenger liners, she was specifically designed to handle the rough seas of the Inside Passage while boasting more luxuries than most ocean liners of her time. First class passengers were treated to fine meals in the 112-seat dining room and enjoyed after dinner drinks in a comfortable social club with maple paneling and a grand piano. A luxurious maple observation deck was also available to all of the passengers. At the helm was a respected Captain, Louis P. Locke, a man who knew the waters of the Inside Passage well and was respected by all. Locke was in a hurry that night, as they were already running three hours behind schedule, but making up that time gradually over the journey should not have been a problem. On the surface, even behind schedule, it seemed like just another routine run south at the end of the season. But the Inside Passage has a way of turning on you fast, and an early winter snow was falling.

Though the Inside Passage is spared the brunt of the vicious northern Pacific storms with numerous barrier islands to the west, the winter can produce gale-force north winds and blinding snowstorms quite unexpectedly. Within an hour of the 10 p.m. Skagway departure, the snow and wind had increased significantly. At Battery Point, sixteen miles south of Skagway, the winds were recorded at fifty miles per hour, and the snow had reduced visibility to just beyond the bow of the ship. This weather pattern is common for October, so Captain Locke and his crew stayed their normal course. When visual navigation was rendered impossible by conditions, the crew had to rely on navigational charts, compass readings and the bouncing the echo of the ship's horn off of the mountains to establish their location and to avoid the treacherous reefs in the canal.

The reefs and rocks found just below the surface of the Inside Passage were not always submerged. In fact, just 10,000 years ago when the seas were 300-400 feet lower than they are today, some were mountainous islands. Many former islands now lie well below the surface of the water and are merely excellent fishing spots known only to the salmon and halibut fishers of Southeast Alaska. Some of these sit just below sea level and are now considered partially submerged reefs, arising from the surface twice a day during low tides. In a semi-diurnal tidal zone like the Inside Passage, tidal swings can change the level of the ocean by as much as thirty feet, making seemingly safe water in high tide very treacherous. The sometimes-underwater reefs boast sheets of jagged rock, rendering them capable of reducing a ship's hull to fragments in seconds. Most of them were noted on navigational charts by 1918 and almost all had buoys attached to them to serve as a visual warning to approaching vessels. In the extremely low visibility of a night like October 23rd, an unlit buoy marking the hazard would have been all but useless. It was just such a buoy that marked Vanderbilt Reef.

Vanderbilt Reef rises up 1,000 feet from the bottom of the Lynn Canal. Encompassing about one-half of an acre and mostly underwater at high tide, this table top-shaped reef is located in the middle of a narrow point in the Lynn Canal and sits twelve feet above the surface of the water at high tide. It is not known how the captain and the pilot got off the suggested course. Perhaps there was an error taking compass bearings, perhaps the rough seas pushed the *Sophia* off course. Whatever the cause, the *Sophia* deviated west of the charted route at some point. At 2 a.m., the eleven-knot speed of the vessel was abruptly halted to the horrifying sound of metal scraping on rock. The passengers, who were mostly asleep in their bunks, were hurled from bed and into their worst fears. The propellers continued to turn and churn for a few more seconds before they died out. Then, all that could be heard was the howling of wind, the crashing of waves and the screams of the doomed passengers.

The ship was stuck atop the reef with no hope of removing itself from the tiny rock island surround by 1,000-foot deep icy water. An SOS call went out, and ships from around the area prepared for rescue immediately. Captain Locke assessed the ship's hull and informed both the concerned passengers and coming ships that the damage was not catastrophic. Though the ship was indeed stuck, the double hull held up and the boilers were still functioning. Locke hoped the approaching high tide would help the ship extract itself from this predicament. He ordered all passengers and crew to remain on the boat, to wait out the weather until help could arrive.

What we know of the situation on the *Sophia* following its crash comes to us from observations made by crewmembers of the rescue vessels and from letters found on the recovered bodies. After striking the reef, life jackets were issued to the passengers, who were instructed to dress warmly pending the risk of immediate evacuation of the ship should she founder on the reef. The crew appears to have done its best to maintain calm, and the hardy northern passengers took their precarious situation in stride.

Things went back to somewhat normal. The social club piano was heard playing well into the night, and the steam-powered lights burned through many a portal. While certainly not a jovial atmosphere, it seems that the passengers and crew made the best of a bad situation.

By first light, conditions had only worsened, and the high tide did nothing to dislodge the ship. Still, throughout the day, the piano played and rescuers observed the occasional couple walking arm-in-arm upon the decks until the howling winds beckoned them back inside. By afternoon, the *Cedar* had arrived from the south, and an effort was made to establish a line between the two vessels that able-bodied passengers could use to escape the reef. Unfortunately, the *Cedar* was unable to make anchor, and the effort was in vain. That evening, to the horror of the rescuers, the lights on the *Princess Sophia* suddenly went out. It was assumed that water had reached the boiler room of the ship and sinking was imminent. Yet, that was not yet the case. A steam pipe had ruptured and was quickly repaired. One by one the lights came on and passengers were seen dancing to the music of the piano that had become a welcome auditory distraction from the pounding of waves and the howling of the north wind.

The morning of the 25th was a severe disappointment to all surrounding Vanderbilt Reef. The weather had taken a turn for the worse and was now considered a full-force gale. Visibility was near zero, and the poor unfortunates aboard the *Princess Sophia* were horrified by the constant metallic grindings and creaks coming from below. Repeated attempts to unload the passengers were canceled, as they had been for days, because of the horrible conditions. It seemed as if she would founder at any time, but the angry seas prevented any hope of escape. There was no piano music heard that day, and by mid-afternoon the rescue vessels had no choice but to take safe harbor in nearby inlets. This would be the last time anyone saw the *Princess Sophia* above water.

At 4:50 p.m., the *Sophia's* radio operator sent out a desperate plea for assistance: "Ship foundering on reef, come at once." The *Cedar* immediately set out valiantly into the storm to do what it could, but the conditions were so horrendous that to attempt rescue would have been fatal. Thirty minutes later a final message was sent from the radio room: "For God's sake hurry… the water is coming into my room… you talk to me so I know you are coming." The message fell upon ears of the helpless. The *Princess Sophia* was sinking, and there was nothing anyone could do to help. For forty long hours she had sat upon Vanderbilt Reef, and for forty long hours the passengers and crewmembers were forced to face the possibility of the worst-case scenario, which was now a frightful reality.

The strong northern wind and waves combined with the high tide had caused the ship to turn an almost complete 180 degrees on the reef. Following the turn, the ship began slipping down, slowly taking in icy waters. It is estimated that about an hour went by from the initial call for help to her sinking, as most of the watches found with the deceased stopped at 5:50 p.m. The slow process of her descent off the reef had shredded the hull to an almost non-existent state and released all of the ships oil into the surrounding waters. Water rushed in to the boiler room, causing a large explosion that destroyed much of the deck.

Perhaps this is the reason that a large number of passengers were found in their cabins below deck, unable to escape from the now destroyed lower levels of the ship. Several lifeboats were launched, but none made it to shore afloat. Those who did get to the boats were quickly thrown into the waters surrounding the reef, as were those panicked masses that took to the sea in their life jacket. The icy waters would render those floating in them dead within minutes because of exposure alone, but it was not the cold that took the many of the victims. The initial shock of entering frigid water invariably causes one to gasp in shock and pain reflexively. The oil slick that surrounded the doomed vessel was breathed in by at least 160 of the 162 victims recovered and brought into Juneau, suffocating them to death before the elements could claim them.

The tragedy of the *Princess Sophia* crippled the region. Many of her best and brightest were aboard on that fateful day, and many of the dreams and desires of the Klondike went down with her. The community in Dawson has never fully recovered. Though the memory of the Inside Passage's greatest maritime tragedy has been largely overshadowed globally by the horrors of World War I and the infamous sinking of the *Titanic* six years earlier, here in the Last Frontier many families still living in this region have a story of an ancestor lost that night.

The *Sophia* still sits in her grave on Vanderbilt Reef. Accessible to divers, it is a popular spot to explore, though the ravages of the sea and time have caused deterioration. What remains of the ship will soon be gone, but something appears to linger above the surface, reminding seafarers to this day that they are not alone on those waters.

For years following the disaster, ocean-goers have reported seeing strange lights without purpose in the vicinity of Vanderbilt Reef and strange sounds floating over the canal. A longtime friend and respected fisherman of the region tells of such a story that occurred in the late eighties. "Bill," as I will call him, has chosen to remain anonymous for fear of ridicule from fellow fisherman. The events surrounding his sighting scared this brave sourdough to the point that he has given up fishing the waters adjacent to the reef unless absolutely necessary.

It was a calm July evening, bathed in the eternal twilight of an Alaska summer night, when Bill encountered a situation quite unexpected. Bill is a quiet man, a man of the land and a man of simple truth and profound observation. He is the type of fellow that only speaks when necessary, but when he speaks everyone listens. He knows the Lynn Canal like most know their backyard, and his quiet hours with his son aboard their salmon fishing vessel have always been his happiest and most peaceful. This was not the case that July.

Following a long day's hard work, Bill pulled into a bay several miles away from Vanderbilt Reef to catch a much-needed nap before returning to his fishing grounds. The reef is now, as it was then, marked by a large navigation beacon and has been shaved down considerably from its appearance in 1918. As Bill took in the dwindling light, something on the horizon caught his attention. There in the distance toward Vanderbilt Reef he saw what he could only describe as a row of lights, like the portals of a ship fixed in place. Immediately fearing the worst, Bill pulled his anchor and headed out toward the lights, thinking that perhaps another ship had foundered on the reef. Could it be the ferry that was due? He took to his radio calling out to whoever was there as he sped out, his view of the reef now obstructed by an island at the mouth of the bay. There was no response. Repeated calls went unanswered, and Bill traveled as fast as he could toward the opening of the inlet. He knew the *Princess Sophia's* story well, and his thoughts went immediately to the logistics of removing all of the doomed passengers should it be a ferry. Luckily, fishing season was in its prime and fishing vessels were everywhere.

As his boat finally cleared the island, Bill was horrified to realize the lights that had first alarmed him were no longer visible. The ship he had so clearly seen stuck on the reef must have foundered. He put the motor into high gear, calling out a general mayday for what he could only surmise was a now completely submerged vessel. Within minutes, and a hundred yards away from the reef, he abruptly stopped his boat. There was no debris in the water. There were no bodies bobbing on the surface. There was nothing. Surely someone or something from the vessel would be visible, at least an oil slick. But there was nothing except for the gentle lapping of the waves upon the rock on this calm summer evening. He shuddered with the realization that what he thought was a rescue may in fact have been something much different. He had not been sleeping well and was exhausted after a long day's hard work. Was he seeing things, or had he become party to something beyond explanation?

He approached the reef and beamed a light into the water. Nothing was visible; nothing had changed. With a shaking hand and a desire for a good night's sleep or some strong coffee to put at ease what was obviously his overly tired mind, he opened the door to his cabin. It was then that he heard it. Behind him, coming from the direction of Vanderbilt Reef as clear as day, he heard the unmistakable sounds of a piano playing a lively ragtime tune. The fjords have a way of traveling sounds long distances, so Bill's first inclination was that someone had responded to his distress signal and was approaching while listening to the radio. He was embarrassed that he would soon have to explain how his overly tired mind and overactive imagination had fooled him. He would be a laughing stock.

He turned to face the direction of the sound, but to his horror there was nobody there. For miles in every direction, the sea was empty save for the floating sounds of that ragtime tune. Not being one to believe in ghosts, he quickly went to his own ship's radio to see what station the tune was playing on. Between Skagway and Juneau, only a few radio stations can be received, so it did not take him long to realize that the music wasn't coming from the speakers. He went back out on the deck and still the ragtime tune was playing. Bill suddenly got the feeling he was not entirely alone in the waters surrounding Vanderbilt Reef. With haste, he revved up his engine and returned to safe harbor and a pull of whiskey. He noted how strange it was that nobody answered his mayday call. Surely anyone in the immediate vicinity should have heard it and come to his aid—but nobody did.

Bill is not alone in hearing such strange sounds. Another friend, let's call her "Belle," had worked in the cruise industry for more than thirty years. Recently retired, we spoke on her last voyage up the Inside Passage about ghosts in the region when she imparted a story from her early days sailing in the Lynn Canal. A native of nearby Haines, Alaska, she had grown up in the waters of the Northern Lynn Canal and knew them as well as anyone. During this part of her tenure, she was tasked with working as a bartender, but seeing that nobody was there, she decided to step outside for a cigarette and take in the night sky. She could see the light from Vanderbilt Reef in the distance and, as she was accustomed when she passed it, said a little prayer to herself for the souls lost that fateful day in 1918. Scarcely had she finished her prayer when she heard a horrendous creak and groan, as if "a building was collapsing on itself" followed by a chorus of wails and screams.

She looked out into the black night but could see nothing except the faint glow from the navigational buoy on the reef. She ran back inside to sound the general alarm, finding quickly a deckhand with a radio and told him of what she heard. Within an instant, the captain was told and searchlights were scouring the water as a rescue boat was lowered. The mayday was quickly accompanied by the halting of the ship. In the silence, Belle and the deckhand could hear the desperate wails and metallic rumble carrying over the breeze. She feared the worst, but despite the unmistakable noises, the searchlights were unable to locate anything out of the ordinary. A rescue vessel was dispatched to search the waters surrounding the reef but it, too, found nothing askew and it too returned empty handed. The captain was extremely distressed at what he viewed was a false alarm, and if Belle didn't have the assurances of the deckhand that he'd heard the same wails, she thinks she likely would have lost her job. In her more than thirty years on the sea she had seen many a strange thing, but none affected her more than the eerie noises that emanated from Vanderbilt Reef that night.

Belle has always been open to the possibility of ghosts and was certainly aware of the history of the region and the horrors of the sinking of the *Princess Sophia.* But until that night, she had never expected to be so haunted by the past. Never again would she be found on the deck as the ferry passed Vanderbilt Reef, and never again did she say a prayer when the ferry sailed by for fear of rousing those who are not able to rest.

Last traces of the Princess Sophia wreck.
Winter and Pond. Photo Collection, courtesy Alaska State Library.

Interior of Jeff "Soapy" Smith's Parlor, Jefferson R. Smith and Rev. Charles Bowers at the bar.

Wickersham State Historic Sites Photo Collection P87-[no.], courtesy Alaska State Library.

The Spirit of Soapy Smith

There have been several ghostly encounters around Skagway that involve the life and death of Jefferson Randolph "Soapy" Smith. From his infamous parlor to the location of his final resting place, Soapy's spirit haunts the town in many more ways than myth and memory.

The colors of the coastal mountains surrounding Skagway are constantly changing. The vibrant hues of spring and summer almost overnight give way to the creeping dullness of fall, which then submits to the endless march of winter and her ice-shrouded mask. In the six-month winter, one must be a keen observer to take in the tiny shifts of light and color that illuminate the granite empire surrounding the town. The summer's green of the newborn saplings, the rich purple of the fireweed, the yellow of the retreating cottonwood, and the steely blue of the glaciers on a windswept morning are a landscape painter's dream. It takes a special eye, however, to find the beauty in the details of the same view in the coldest times and the darkest months. It takes that same discerning eye—that acceptance of not black or white but never ending shades of gray—to truly understand the story behind one of Skagway's most famous residents. For you see, Soapy Smith's life was never black and white. He was a man of good and evil; a man of kindness and ferocity; a man whose own death is shrouded in a mysterious gray fog.

Soapy's arrival to Skagway was the final chapter in a long story of vice, violence and deceit. He was already famous for being the greatest con artist in the American West. He was already known to be as quick with his persuasive tongue as he was with a slight of the hand. But there was a complicated and gentle side to him that is often overshadowed by his evil deeds.

Much like the infamous mob boss Al Capone or the heroin kingpin Frank Lucas, Soapy was well known for his generosity. Whether it was good for business, or perhaps good for the soul, Soapy would regularly donate selflessly to his community. He contributed greatly during his time in Skagway to local churches and helped finance the town's first hospital. He was well known for establishing the first animal shelter and ultimately saving the lives of many cast-away dogs and horses that would have otherwise died from harsh treatment and weather. Even his victims received his generosity. Many travelers who lost everything to a false claim, a rigged game or a robbery perpetrated by Soapy's henchman would find themselves confronted by the kindly southern gentleman, who was all too happy to give unlucky travelers the fare for a one-way passage out of town. Of course, this also conveniently rid him of a potential problem down the road.

In order to truly understand the complicated antagonist of this gold rush legend, Soapy's story must start at his beginning. Jefferson Randolph Smith was born into antebellum Georgia aristocracy during the fall of 1860. His birth coincided with the end of his family's way of life, as he was brought into the world right before the outbreak of the American Civil War. As the grandson of a wealthy plantation owner and the son of a lawyer, education and propriety were as much of his birthright as was his ancestral property. Unfortunately for young Jefferson, the devastating effects of the war rendered his family penniless and destitute, and they were forced to move from their home and begin a new life in Texas. The laws that governed his family in their new home were enforced by carpetbaggers, men from the North who exploited the poverty and desperation of the people of the South after the war. It is not a great stretch of the imagination to see how this product of Southern gentry came to embrace the life of an outlaw. Soapy was quoted several times during his life of crime justifying his actions, honestly believing he was doing no wrong.

By 1879, he had moved to Denver, beginning his life of crime in the West with the same quick games he perfected in Texas: the shell game, three-card Monte and the soap trick that gave him the nickname he reviled. The soap trick was particularly effective and unique to his crew. Soapy or one of his henchmen would set up a small stand in a busy area of town and bark to the crowd of the soap's many wonders. After a while, feigning desperation due to the lack of sales, the con would truly begin. The salesman, usually Soapy himself, would place bills of various denominations up to $100 into the soap wrappers and shuffle them back into the pile. It would take only $1 to enjoy the miracles of this wonder product, but for that time only, customers had the chance to win up to 100 times their money back.

By this time, a crowd would gather with understandable skepticism. Then, from out of the mob, the first brave soul would step forward with his dollar. To the audience's surprise, the man would pull money from the wrapper, waving it in the air for all to see. Before long, a frenzy would ensue. Men were fighting over the right to buy the soap, and the salesman began auctioning his stock off to the highest bidder. Amidst the joyous cries of the winners were the howls of those willing to pay double or more for their chance. What the crowd didn't know was that the men winning money were not aimless passersby, but in fact Soapy's gang. Before the crowd knew what hit them, the soap was sold off and the gang was long since gone. In a town where the population was recycled on a weekly basis, such a con was extremely profitable.

By 1887, Soapy became one of the first true crime bosses west of the Mississippi and was receiving tribute for most of the criminal activity that occurred within Denver's limits. A lot of his accrued wealth paid off politicians and police in town. In 1888, he opened a saloon and gambling hall called the Tivoli Club, which became his base of operations. From there, his crimes expanded into a diverse array of scams, robberies, racketeering and forgery all under the protection of the government and police.

By 1892, law and order had settled into Denver, and Soapy and the gang sought out a new camp of marks. The town of Creede, Colorado fit perfectly. A large silver strike had occurred in 1892, and the lawless town was ripe for the taking by the ambitious and organized gang. Rolling into town with a large bankroll and a small army of beautiful Denver prostitutes, it did not take long for the gang to overpower the ruling merchant class. Soapy was again the criminal boss of an upstart mining camp. He was even able to secure a deputy sheriff post for his brother-in-law, guaranteeing little, if any, trouble from the law. It was in Creede that Soapy became famous for his role as a town benefactor. This was a contemporary criminal mastermind, a boss who realized that in order to fleece the people without disruption, he first needed their trust.

As is often the case in boomtowns, mines became played out and soon the rush was over. It was no matter. The gang packed up its earnings and headed back to Denver, which was enjoying resurgence of lawlessness and vice. With an army of corrupt politicians already in his services, and years of experience under his belt, Soapy was soon in control again. His activities in Denver continued unabated until the election of Governor Davis Hanson Waite, who ordered that gambling halls, saloons and brothels of Denver be closed and called for the removal of the corrupt politicians that had choked progress in city hall for so long. Soapy's support structure vanished, and by 1896 it was time to move on. Though he tried to make several towns his home, including one in Mexico, nothing was the right fit. Lucky for him, another boomtown was just about to become known to the world.

Almost overnight, the towns of Skagway and Dyea were born as the gateway to the fabled riches of the interior. Soapy's gang headed there in 1897 and they soon realized they stumbled upon a bunko operators dream. The trails in Skagway and Dyea leading to the interior were teaming with thousands of men in a desperate rush to get to the gold fields as quickly possible. By the end of the rush, more than 100,000 people used Skagway or Dyea as their route to the interior. Few of these men and women had the time to stay in these towns any longer than it took to get supplies. Fewer still were likely to complain about any minor con games they were victim to, as the lawlessness of early mining towns prevailed and little could be done for such offenses.

The gang soon fell into familiar and well-worn treads. By mid-winter, Soapy's men had paid off what little law was present, and generous donations to local churches, hospitals and charitable organizations had much of Skagway and Dyea willing to overlook the burgeoning criminal enterprises of the gang. Smith and his men found themselves perfectly situated to rule an empire of vice and crime in the North. The gang assumed many faces and identities in the town, all of which were typically fronts to conceal a vast and sophisticated criminal atmosphere. Unsuspecting prospectors fresh off the boat would be sized up and befriended by men posing as newspaperman, men of God, merchants, fellow prospectors, gamblers and a host of other reputable members of frontier society. Once under their trust, these new arrivals were skirted away into one of many of the bunko games and cons designed to separate the men from their money.

Before long, Soapy purchased the building where the First

Bank of Skagway was located and converted it into Jeff. Smith's Parlor. The parlor offered fine cigars, spirits and oysters as well as a back parlor lavishly decorated with fake palm trees and electric light. Behind the building was a fenced in lot with a stuffed bald eagle. It was here that Soapy ran his criminal empire. Many an unwary prospector found himself gambling away his grubstake in one of the rigged games of the parlor or headed to the back "see the eagle"—a euphemism for the robberies that took place in the back lot. A curious traveler, often plied generously with drinks, would head back to the stuffed eagle where he was knocked over the head and robbed. By the time he came to his senses, the robber had slipped away into the night via a trap door on the fence. It seemed as if the foxes were destined to rule the roost forever in Skagway, but a group of residents were quietly brewing with resentment and frustration, waiting for their chance to sit atop the mountain of money coming into the valley.

The Committee of 101 was formed as a counterpoint to the organized gang of outlaws, and it was made up of merchants, real estate salesman, packers and other residents whose businesses were hurting because of crime. After a year of lawlessness, the Committee of 101 decided it was time for a change. On March 8, 1898, in a public display of power, the committee posted a letter of warning to the criminals of Skagway:

> Warning! A word to the wise should be sufficient! All Confidence, Bunco and Sure-thing Men, And all other objectionable characters are notified to leave Skaguay and White pass Road Immediately. And to remain away. Failure to comply with this warning will be followed by prompt action. 101.

The warning did not go unnoticed by Soapy. Within days he amassed a group of more than three hundred supporters and posted this response:

ANSWER TO WARNING

> The body of men styling themselves 101 are hereby notified that any overt act committed by them will be promptly met by the Law abiding Citizens of Skaguay and each member and HIS PROPERTY will be held responsible for any unlawful act on their part and the law and order society consisting of 317 citizens will see that Justice is dealt out to its full extent as no Blackmailers or Vigilantes will be tolerated. The Committee.

After reading that, the Committee of 101 reluctantly stepped back into the shadows of discontent, and business as usual carried on. Soapy's power and prestige continued to grow within the town. On July 7, 1898, three days after Soapy rode at the head of Skagway's 4th of July parade as grand marshal for his good deeds, a man named John D. Stewart arrived in Skagway after a successful trip to the Dawson gold fields. He was carrying on him an estimated $3,000 in gold dust and, unfortunately, a trusting heart. After securing his fortune in the Mondamin Hotel, Stewart ran into two of Soapy's henchman: John Bowers and James "Slim-Jim" Foster.

The two men learned of Stewart's poke and its location, and before long, they convinced Stewart to take the money to a local bank rather than leave it in the untrustworthy hotel. They took him to meet the banker and helped to examine the safe before entrusting the establishment with his money. Before reaching the bank, the group ran into two more of Soapy's men who were engaged in a game of Three-card Monte. Stewart joined in, and after winning several rounds he soundly became convinced he could run the tables with the rest of his hard earned money that was in his hotel. He quickly fetched it and, in due time, found himself losing a significant portion of his fortune. Realizing he was being taken advantage of, Stewart refused to pay the money he owed. Before he knew what was happening the four men subdued and robbed him of the entire $3,000 worth of gold dust.

Stewart complained to the Marshall, but was greeted with an indifference to the predicament because he was paid off by Soapy and not apt to get back money for a man who lost it in a game of chance. But Stewart, who was well known and well liked, complained to anyone who would listen. The Committee of 101 had grown in size and saw this as its chance to overtake the gang and gain control of the town. The members were up in arms over the theft, and a large crowd soon demanded the return of the money from Soapy himself. Soapy was undeterred in his convictions. He insisted that Stewart had lost the money fair and square and stood behind his men, challenging anyone who dared to try and take it. A line was drawn in the sand, and trouble was brewing for the outlaws of Skagway.

Throughout the night and into the next day the Committee of 101 held meetings about avenging the theft. The town, which only days before had regarded Soapy as a hero, was turning against the "King of the Frontier Con-Men" and his constituents. Soapy sensed the end was near and decided to do something he hardly ever did—he became extremely drunk. By the night of July 8, he was in a stupor. Geographically, there were only two ways out of town. One was over the passes to the north, a journey fraught with toil and peril. The second route was by sea, and the easiest way to escape the mob. Unfortunately, that route was blocked by the mob, which was meeting at the Juneau Company Wharf deciding what to do. At 9 p.m., a newspaperman came to Soapy's Parlor and told him the crowd was preparing to turn on the gang and remove them from town for good. Enraged, Soapy grabbed his rifle and marched toward the wharf to confront the mob.

The entrance to the Juneau Company Wharf was guarded by

four men, one of whom was Frank Reid. The men were instructed by the committee to ensure neither Soapy nor any of his men disrupt the proceedings. What happened next is unclear, and has been a matter of controversy and conjecture ever since. What happened next could be the root cause of the hauntings reported in the area, as there is a distinct chance the murderer continued to walk free through Skagway well after the conclusion of this deadly affair.

What is known is that Soapy bypassed three of the four guards and walked directly up to Frank Reid. Soapy, in a drunken state, attempted to hit Frank with the rifle. Frank blocked the blow with his forearm and tried to wrestle control of the weapon from Soapy's grip. The scuffle escalated, and Reid drew his pistol. The last thing Jefferson Randolph Smith ever said while alive was, "For God's sake, don't shoot!" The plea went unheeded, and Frank Reid fired. The first shot in his revolver was a faulty cartridge and didn't go off, but the subsequent rounds hit true. Soapy crumpled to the ground with rifle in hand either before or just after firing on Reid. Eyewitness accounts estimate that between five and nine shots were fired. Soapy was wounded in the left arm and thigh and received a fatal shot directly to the heart. Reid was wounded in the lower abdomen and groin.

Soapy died almost instantly, while Reid languished on for twelve torturous days. The final seconds of this brief and deadly standoff have been speculated over since it took place. Many believe it was another of the four guards, a White Pass & Yukon Route employee named Jesse Murphy, who killed Soapy. Murphy allegedly ran over to the two men fighting once the shots rang out, wrestled the rifle away from the wounded Smith and shot Soapy directly in the heart. Some say the incident was credited to Reid because his wounds were mortal and a claim of self-defense justified killing Soapy; whereas Murphy would have been guilty of murder and sentenced to death. The White Pass & Yukon Route was an important part of Skagway's future, as it transported people and gold to and from Dawson City. Had one of its employees been found guilty of murder, unnecessary complications would have arisen in the building of the railroad, and capitalism was king in this land.

Within a few seconds of the shooting, some of Soapy's men ran over to help him, but they were greeted by Murphy wielding Soapy's weapon, promising a quick death to those who came any further. The gang dispersed into the night, while committee members went to Reid's aid. Another guard grabbed Reid's pistol, which lay underneath him, and noted in writing that the gun was empty save for two spent shells and one unexploded cartridge—one bullet short of the three that had struck Smith. On July 20, 1898 Frank Reid died from his wounds. He was given a hero's burial in the Skagway City Cemetery with the entire town there to celebrate his life and mourn his death. To this day, the lavish headstone marking the savior of Skagway's mortal remains still stands. Twenty yards away, just outside the historic cemetery's gates, Soapy was interred in a pauper's grave. Legend has it that only one mourner, purported to be his mistress, wept at the foot of his earthly resting place the day of his burial.

In the years since the shootout at the Juneau Company Wharf, Skagway has changed. The boomtown of 10,000 residents was reduced to 1,000 by 1901. Except for a brief influx of troops in World War II, it has remained a small railroad town for much of the time since. The exception to that rule takes place every summer when cruise ships bring upwards of 1,000,000 tourists to the town every year to bask in its beauty, history, and its many adventures. Naturally, no history of a gold rush boomtown is complete without an outlaw and a shootout, and the tale of Frank Reid and Soapy Smith has become the stuff of legend.

Today you can not only visit the final resting places of Reid and Soapy, but you can also find a historical marker showing the exact spot where the deadly duel took place and pass by the very building where Soapy Smith held court and fleeced newcomers of their purse in 1898. In fact, the Jeff. Smith Parlor was moved in the 1960s from its original location on 6th Avenue between Broadway and State streets to just off of Second Avenue and Broadway Street—mere yards from the site of the Juneau Company Wharf shooting. It is in these three places that reports of unexplained phenomena have occurred, and it is from these structures and grounds that Soapy continues to reach us from beyond the grave.

The first time I heard about an encounter with Soapy's ghost, it was told to me by a Minnesota couple accompanying me on a hiking and rafting expedition several years ago. Virginia and Bud Knudson appeared, for all intents and purposes, the typical clientele I was accustomed to guiding up the historic Chilkoot Trail and down the lazy Taiya River. They were retired, in their early sixties and had spent the past few years exploring North America in an RV, taking the time to enjoy all of the sights afforded to them on the road. They shared a passion for history and were intensely interested in any and all information I could give them about Skagway during the gold rush. They were my favorite kind of clients: bright, passionate, and eager to engage me in their theories regarding the regions vast and varied history. Naturally, before too long in our conversation, the subject of Soapy Smith came up. I was surprised at how little they knew of him, being that it was such a pertinent focus of much of the histories typically passed onto tourists in this town. I was all too happy to relay to them the tales I had read.

Following the tour, I invited them to accompany me to the sites of major events in Soapy's life and demise. On my way back into town, I grabbed several laminated photos of Skagway at the time, as well as a picture of Soapy himself. The photo showed him standing next to the bar in his parlor. After we headed to the grave site, I took them to the Jeff. Smith's Parlor building. At the time, it was under renovation by its new owners, the National Park

Service. I took the opportunity to relay to them some tales of my time working underneath the structure as the park archaeologist. I passed them the photographs of Soapy, of his parlor in its former location, and of the Juneau Wharf as it looked in 1898. As they passed the photos among each other, I proceeded to tell them one of my most popular stories about the building, regarding the only unexplained phenomena I had ever personally encountered here in Skagway. I had not yet gotten through the story when Bud, quite uncharacteristically, interrupted me.

"What is this, some kind of prank you guys pull on tourists?" he said, obviously concerned. I assured him that I had no idea what he was talking about.

"We just saw this guy last night. How do you make this photo look so old?" He chuckled, convinced that he had outsmarted a con-man of the new generation.

It took quite some assurance to convince him that I was not pulling a fast one and that, indeed, this was a photo of Soapy. Before I had convinced Bud, I saw that Virginia looked rather pale and ill and invited them to sit on a nearby bench while we talked. Bud informed me that they had arrived later in the evening the night before and headed out to a commonly used RV park down by the shore. The park was full for the evening, as it was well into the peak of our summer season, so they headed back into town toward another RV park in the center of town. It was still light outside, for in the peak of summer it never becomes fully dark, when they passed a man that caught their attention.

He was dressed distinctly in period clothing—a three-piece suit complete with watch and chain—and on his shoulder he carried some kind of rifle. They naturally assumed he was a local that worked in one of the shows in town and slowed down to ask him where they could find the park. For whatever reason, be it rudeness or drunkenness or sheer exhaustion, the man did not turn to look at them and instead kept walking south at a brisk pace toward the water in a stumbling stupor. Commenting on how he was likely drunk, they chuckled and continued on their way. Seconds later they heard the distinct sounds of gunshots or fireworks to the south.

Looking through their rear view mirrors, they saw a hazy blue smoke in a small park far behind them. It was not too far off from the Fourth of July at the time, so they assumed that it was simply some kids setting off the rest of their fireworks and drove on into the night, eager to get some shut eye before their big day. They thought nothing more of it until I showed them the picture. It was now I that felt I was being conned, so I asked them to take me to where they saw the man. The actual site of Soapy's shooting was less than a block from where we were sitting, but I wanted to see if they were telling the truth, so I loaded them into my van and drove in the opposite direction.

"Is this where you saw him?" I asked as we passed a park that had been under water during that time.

"No," Bud said, "It's closer to the other side of town."

I then drove, rather hurriedly, to where I knew Soapy had taken his last walk down State Street. As soon as we pulled onto the road, Virginia noticed the grocery store and rather excitedly yelled that this was the location they had seen the man, just a few blocks south not far from a gas station. This, I informed the couple, was indeed the route that Soapy had taken on his final walk in life and that most people would have been unaware of that fact.

The park where they had seen the blue smoke is the very location a marker sits to this day recording the very spot in which the infamous shooting occurred. We drove past it in silence, stunned at the revelation that would convince all three of us that what they had seen was not of this world. I stopped the vehicle and scoured the park for remnants of exploded fireworks, of which I found none. I climbed back into the car and told them I found nothing, started up the engine and drove slowly away from my amazement and their terror. We continued, without speaking, to a local brewery where several rounds of spruce tip ale had to be consumed before we could speak again of the previous night's events.

Did this couple really see the ghost of Soapy Smith, or was it simply a prank played on an unsuspecting wilderness guide? Is Soapy bound to this earth, convinced that he cannot rest until his real killer is brought to justice? Was what they witnessed merely a matter of coincidence or is there something deeper? I suppose I will never know, but I can say with certainty that Virginia and Bud were either legitimately afraid that afternoon, or they should leave retirement for a career in the theater. Theirs is not the only story surrounding locations involving Soapy Smith. As I alluded to earlier, I myself had a strange encounter while working alone in Jeff. Smith's Parlor one summer evening that, to this day, I cannot explain and remains the only unexplained phenomena I have ever experienced.

From the summer of 2011 through the summer of 2012, I served as a Park archaeologist for Klondike Gold Rush National Park in Skagway. During my tenure, one of my main projects was to complete a thorough analysis of the ground beneath the current location of Soapy's parlor in order to allow the National Park Service to completely restore it without damaging anything of historical importance now below ground. The parlor was moved from its original location on 6th Avenue, between Broadway and State streets by George Rapuzzi, who ran a gold rush museum in the building, which he inherited from Skagway tourism pioneer Marten Itjen. The structure itself had been significantly altered from the days of its use as Soapy's den of inequity.

The fenced-in rear of the building with the trap door was long since gone. The interior of the structure had served multiple uses following the demise of Soapy and his gang, such as the location of several of Frank Clancy's saloons and restaurants in

1898, and eventually was known as the Sans Souci Restaurant and Oyster Parlor. By 1899, it had come into the ownership of the Skagway Hook and Ladder Company Fire Department and was used for storage. Eventually, in about 1935, it was converted by Itjen into the Jeff. Smith's Parlor Museum. The museum boasted several taxidermy bull moose with horns locked in a defiant struggle, a taxidermy sled dog, the original mahogany bar where Soapy held court, as well as several animatronic characters that would point a gun or raise a drink toward patrons as they entered the property.

In 1963, the building was moved by then-owner George Rapuzzi to bring it closer into the downtown tourist district. Rapuzzi restored much of the building to Itjen's 1935 design and continued his work furthering tourism in Skagway. Following Rapuzzi's own death in 1986, the museum was closed—seemingly for good. However, the entirety of his estate passed to his niece, Phyllis Brown, who in turn sold everything, including Jeff. Smith's Parlor, to the National Park Service in 2007. It was the Park Service's intention that such an important building be preserved for future generations to learn from and enjoy. After much debate, it was determined that the building would be restored not to the appearance of Soapy's parlor in its heyday, but rather to be a representation of Marten Itjen's museum with an in-depth look into the history of Skagway's tourism. What had been once deadly ground for the unwary and an actual den of thieves was destined to become a museum of a museum.

Initial research on the 2nd Avenue lot the building now sits on produced little historical significance in regard to the gold rush. The area had been in the muddy, often underwater, tidal flats in 1898 and well into the twentieth century, and therefore had been barely utilized prior to the filling in of the landscape in World War II. Photographic evidence indicates that in the heyday of the gold rush, an open-air storage area was on the property that was used for hay and lumber. Excavations produced several sporadic dumping episodes underneath and next to the structure. Some of the artifacts found there were consistent with the gold rush or just after, but most appeared to be from the World War II period or later. Unfortunately, almost all of the artifacts found were mixed together regardless of age. This meant that they had most likely been re-deposited from somewhere else in town and were therefore of little consequence scientifically and historically. There was the occasionally a spectacular museum quality piece like a toothbrush with a Seattle hotel's name still on it or an unbroken whiskey bottle straight from the turn of the 20th century, but what remained there of substance was largely out of context. I soon found out, however, that it was not only the refuse of yesteryear that remained on this lot.

The first odd happenings on the lot were simple enough. It all started with a missing bag here, or a misplaced tool there. Things would turn up in places they simply should not have been. A trowel, of paramount importance in our excavations, disappeared for several days only to turn up in the very pit we were in the process of excavating. An artifact bag, carefully labeled and waiting for historical treasures, would end up missing and presumed blown away only to be found inside the parlor where it could not have moved by itself.

Finally, and most alarmingly given its expense and value, a camera full of all of the pictures recording our excavation process went missing from the building. I was at my wits end—surely the loss of the camera was due to a thief jumping the locked fence at night—and I chided myself for being so stupid as to leave something so valuable in an unlocked building. After searching high and low well past the end of the workday, I could only conclude that it was stolen and gone forever. In desperation, I stood where the bar once was and exclaimed how much I needed a drink, laughingly saying the round would be on me if that camera showed up tomorrow. I then proceeded outside and closed the crude wooden door, placing an unassuming piece of tape over the door jam. Ever the detective, I surmised that if the looter returned in the night, I would know that they had come. I then headed home, tail tucked between my legs, and planned ways to avoid my boss for the next several months.

In the morning, I returned to the building, unlocked the gate that surrounded the property and went to the structure. The tape, I noticed, had not been touched at all. It was situated at the bottom of the door, and the unlit lot in the dark of the fall Alaskan night would have rendered it invisible. But despite it being untouched, as sure as the sun shines, inside the building was the camera. It sat in its case right where the bar Soapy once ruled. A thin layer of dust covered it, as if it had sat for some time. A shock of cold ran through me as if I had jumped into a tub of ice water. I had literally stood right there just the night before, pleading for its safe return.

I knew I was overworked, but there is no way I could have been so exhausted as to have missed such an obvious location. It was completely fine save for dead batteries. As I stared at in amazement, the door to the building slammed shut, the revolving wooden propeller that secured it in place sliding down and sealing it.

I do not know to this day if it was just the famous Skagway wind or if the borrower of the camera from beyond the grave wanted their promised drink and did their best to keep me to my word. I can say with certainty that I have never run so quickly in my life, nor have I ever felt so justified in purchasing a pint of whiskey and leaving it in an abandoned building. Was this the mischievous ghost of Soapy? It may very well have been, as he was known to not drink frequently and the whiskey remained untouched through the season. Was it the watchful and playful specter of Marten Itjen or George Rapuzzi? Or was it, instead, one of the countless victims of Soapy come back from the dead to reclaim something they had lost, or a ghost occupying the grounds surrounding the new location of the parlor?

The answer, of course, is as unknown as the location of Soapy's bones today. In September of 1919 heavy rains caused Reid Falls, above the cemetery, to spill over its banks and into the graves. Many mortal remains were washed out to sea, including Soapy's. They were never recovered, and to this day a deep gulch occupies where once his final resting place was. Perhaps his restless spirit still wanders due to this final injustice, when the waters named after his murderer sent him forever into the infinite once again.

April 1954, scene of Thomas Bay.
Lloyd H. "Kinky" Bayers Manuscript Collection, courtesy Alaska State Library.

The Bay of Death

Just to the north of Petersburg lies Thomas Bay. Numerous reports of strange, supernatural beasts known as Kushtaka, or the otterman, have been reported in the uninhabited area. Are these half man/half otters the spiritual remnants of a terrible tragedy that occurred in the bay generations ago?

The island community of Petersburg is not often a sought-out destination when traveling to Southeast Alaska. In a landscape where evidence of indigenous people goes back more than 10,000 years, the oldest sites there date only to about 1,000 years ago and seem to indicate a seasonal visitation rather than year round habitation. This inconsistent occupation changed in the late 19th century when a Norwegian named Peter Buschmann arrived and constructed docks, a saw mill, and a cannery. By 1910, the town of Petersburg, named after the Norwegian entrepreneur, had become a very successful fishing village. Attracting enough Scandinavian immigrants to be known as "Little Norway," the town now boasts numerous canneries, a large fishing fleet and a per capita income that has been ranked among the highest in North America. Tourism is largely restricted to the wealthy, with yacht owners and small cruise ships sailing into port during the summer months, taking advantage of the authentic experience provided by a lack of large scale tourist economy. Just to the north of Petersburg there is a bay devoid of the small fishing village's vibrancy; a place where bird song is muted and the rustling in the bushes is usually just the wind. This remote wilderness is now officially known as Thomas Bay, but to locals it is commonly referred to as the Bay of Death.

Little evidence can be found of the tragedy unleashed upon this bay in 1750. What is known is that, because of steep and unpredictable slopes and wet weather commonplace in Southeast Alaska, an entire Tlingit village was buried in a massive landslide. More than five hundred people were killed during the disaster, and the bay has been thought of as cursed ever since. Even today, the mortal remains of the villagers rest below tons of mountain rubble in this lonely and isolated landscape. Or do they? Reports of strange beasts and even stranger disappearances abound in this part of the state and perhaps tie into not only the afterlife of these poor unfortunates, but also to a half-man half-otter beast steeped in myth and legend.

Kushtaka are mythical ottermen spoken of for generations among the Tlingit and Tsimshian peoples in Southeast Alaska as well as the Dan'aina of South Central Alaska and the Inuit of Northern Alaska. Interestingly, these interior tribes are believed to have had little contact with the Southeastern tribes and have uniquely formed languages and only distant genetic similarities. Such differences make a culturally shared story unlikely. According to the Tlingit, the otterman is a supernatural spirit capable of shape shifting and luring people away from their villages. Once into the woods or out to sea, the otterman will either claw his victims to pieces or, worse yet, transform them into an otterman. If transformed, victims are doomed to wander forever as shape-shifting demons.

The indigenous description of the appearance of these

creatures is fairly consistent. They are shorter than a man, walk on two legs, and have long sharp claws and foul smelling, oozing sores covering their bodies. They more often than not travel in packs and are sometimes spoken of in stories as having villages, canoes and other human cultural traits. Their methods of drawing humans away from their village often involve the mimicking of a child's cry, or the voice of a lost loved one calling in the distance. In some tales, the voice heard is that of a loved one who has been turned into a Kushtaka. Though it possesses supernatural abilities, it is not without its weaknesses. It has been said that dogs will scare away Kushtaka, and they can be harmed by contact with dogs as well as fire, copper and even urine.

Not every tale told of these creatures speaks of them as evil. Many stories tell of sailors hopelessly lost at sea with no land in sight or someone desperately lost in the woods and close to freezing to death being saved by Kushtaka. Their salvation is not without its price, as the human must be turned into an otterman to be saved. Perhaps then, what has been reported in the Bay of Death is a result of the rescue of the long buried village by Kushtaka. Perhaps, the accounts written by Harry D. Colp in "The Strangest Story Ever Told" in 1900 speak not of unknown animals, but rather of the residents of this buried community defending their ancestral territory.

Colp's account is indeed strange when taken out of context, but to believers in otterman, it is just another warning for those choosing to venture out into the wilderness on the own. His tale begins in the mining district of Wrangell when he partnering up with three other prospectors. One of the group, named Charlie, knew of a Native man from the area who had in his possession a piece of gold infused quartz from an unknown location. After much persistence, the man disclosed the supposed location of the find. He had found the rock in a rockslide in the mountains above Thomas Bay. It was a distance of less than fifty miles from where they were. This news sent the men into a golden frenzy. Three of the four started to work right away to raise money for a grubstake, while Charlie set out on a reconnaissance mission in order to ascertain the validity of the claim. Nothing was heard of him for over a month when one day, without any possessions other than his canoe, he arrived exhausted into camp. Disheveled and starving, Charlie asked for a meal threw a large gold-infused quartz rock into the corner with the indifference of a man who was beyond caring about material possessions. As the men ogled the find, Charlie devoured the food and fell into a deep sleep. The next morning he was roused awake to tell of his adventure to the area. He still said not a word of his journey, but instead borrowed some warm clothing and headed out into camp for the day. The men were positively foaming at the mouth for news of his expedition when he arrived again that afternoon. He informed them that he was planning on leaving Alaska the next morning via boat and did not intend to return. If the men agreed to pay his fare, he would tell them what he saw. The story he unfolded was almost too strange to believe.

Charlie had made his way to Thomas Bay and soon had found a suitable place to camp. He was surprised by the lack of any game in the area given the richness of the flora that surrounded him. The silence was unbroken even by the familiar chirp of the ground squirrel in the trees. After a time in the eerily quiet landscape, a storm arrived, and he found himself stuck in his tent for days. Once the weather broke, he scouted the area and identified several landmarks the Native man had spoken about. Gold panning in a nearby creek produced some color and convinced him he was on the right track. Excited for the possibilities ahead, he planned a reconnaissance of the headwaters as soon as possible above the creek. The long travel and poor diet left him exhausted, and he needed some additional strength for the journey. Eight miles distant was a ridge that looked promising for grouse, which is rich in fat and calories. He ventured there the next day.

As luck would have it, there were a few grouse on the ridge, and in short order he shot three. The last fell over the side of the ridge and stopped on a bare stretch of earth one hundred yards below. When he scrambled down to retrieve it he discovered a large piece of quartz laden with gold flecks. Too large to take in total and without the proper equipment for prospecting on him he decided to use the butt of his gun to break some off. Doing so caused the butt of his gun to shatter, rendering it useless. It was no matter, though; soon he was to be rich beyond his wildest dreams and could afford one hundred guns. Charlie covered up the find, took in his surrounding so as to make it easier to find again and started to head down the mountains. What Charlie saw next was indeed strange and unbelievable. Below him, swarming in a mass was a group of beasts. According to Colp, the horrified prospector:

> ...couldn't call them anything but devils, as they were neither men nor monkeys yet they looked like both. They were entirely sexless, their bodies covered with long, coarse hair, except where the scabs and running sores had replaced it.

The "devils" swarmed toward him, letting forth piercing cries. In a terror, he forgot the state of his weapon and aimed it toward the charging creatures, but to no avail. In an instant they were upon him, clawing at his back and shrieking. He wrote that they emitted a foul stench from their bodies and had sores. Perhaps driven to the brink by terror and exhaustion, Charlie lost consciousness. When he came to, he found himself in his canoe, floating in the darkness out in Thomas Bay. He had no idea how long it had been or how he had gotten away. All of his possessions were gone save for his canoe paddles and the large piece of quartz he had found on the ridge. Overcome with a powerful thirst and chilled to the bone, he paddled back to Wrangell exhausted and near death to buy the first ticket he could find out of Alaska.

What did Charlie see out there? Some theorize it was the result of hallucinations brought on by spoiled food. Others have speculated that the man simply had enough of the far north and created the fantastic story to procure a fast ticket home. But what of the gold infused quartz? Why would a gold crazed miner knowingly walk away from such riches without laying claim to the land he found it on? Is it possible that what he encountered was the remnants of the buried Tlingit village, resurrected from the dead, only to be doomed to wander the earth forever as shapeshifting monsters? Unfortunately, to this day, it is unknown where Charlie spent his last days, and the only evidence that remains of his encounter with Kushtaka is Colp's account. Interest in the otterman still remains fervent to this day. In fact, celebrity and actor Charlie Sheen is known to have flown into Sitka in the summer of 2013 for the express purpose of searching for the creature. The search did not produce any results. Perhaps ottermen have a predisposition toward rejecting men named Charlie?

Alaskan Hotel on South Franklin Street, Juneau, Ca. 1913.

Winter and Pond. Photo Collection,
courtesy Alaska State Library.

The Alaskan Hotel

The Alaskan Hotel and Bar is purportedly haunted by the victim of a terrible crime at the hands of her own husband, doomed to walk the halls of her murder for eternity.

In order to understand the city of Juneau, one must begin where so many Alaskan cities began: the quest for gold. The state's capitol was not always the bustling mini-metropolis you see today. Long before the arrival of the Europeans, the indigenous peoples knew the land as Dzántik'i Héeni, or the "Base of the Flounder's River." As the great gold claims of California and the Pacific Northwest petered out, the prospecting culture looked to the north to satisfy its lust for the color. This often windy, snowy, mountain-locked peninsula proved to be just what they were looking for. In the 1870s, prospectors began staking claims below Juneau and all along the coastal mountains of the Inside Passage. The quartz veins inside the granite mountains around the present day city were believed to have a particularly rich gold belt, extending more than eighty miles, from Windham Bay in the south, to Berners Bay in the north.

In 1880, Sitka based mining engineer George Pilz offered grubstakes to any miners interested in pursuing claims in the area.

He also offered large payments in goods to any local natives that could provide evidence of promising land for precious mineral exploration in the territory. Within a short time, a chief by the name of Cowee, whose ancestral lands sat near present day Juneau, brought in a large sample of gold ore. Excited at the possibility of a great claim to the north, Pilz sent miners Richard Harris and Joe Juneau with Cowee to his home on Auke Bay to investigate the chief's claim.

Juneau and Harris were both examples of the classic prospector and pioneer traveling north with dreams of gold. Both were from the east: Juneau coming from the Canadian province of Quebec, and Harris coming from Ireland and educated in Philadelphia. Both were dreamers, both were searchers, and, rumor has it, both were big drinkers. The initial trip produced little for the men but hangovers. Both Juneau and Harris traded the bulk of the grubstake Pitz had given them for Native hoochinoo, a spirituous liquor that the Tlingit distilled from potatoes. Upon their return, Pitz sent them back to the area, assuring harsh consequences if his orders were not followed to a tee. This trip proved to be much more fruitful. On October 3, 1880, Cowee led the men to an area that Harris would call the Silver Bow Basin, named after a lucrative mine in Montana. What they saw would start a frenzy of men and activity that continues to this day.

"We followed the gulch down from the summit of the mountain into the basin," Harris later said. "And it was a beautiful sight to see, the large pieces of quartz, spangled over with gold." Their initial explorative work in Gold Creek brought almost 1,000 pounds of gold ore back to Sitka. The rush was on.

Miners poured into the district. On October 18, 1880, Harris and Juneau staked out a 160-acre town site on the beach and it very quickly became a full-fledged boomtown. They named it Harrisburgh, but in due time the name was changed to Rockwell after Lt. Com. Charles Rockwell, the American naval commander, whose detachment kept order in the remote mining camp. Rumor has it the name change was because of the amount of towns named Harrisburgh already existing in the United States. The name Rockwell was not to last, however. On December 14, 1881 the name Juneau won a vote by the miners. Allegedly, Juneau plied those who voted for his name with ample hoochinoo and white man's whiskey.

In the years following, the first town settled in American Alaska grew in fame and importance. The Silver Gulch mine continued to produce color, and other operations opened on nearby Douglas Island. Now-famous diggings like the Alaska-Juneau, Treadwell, and the Ready-Bullion mines would produce hundreds of millions of dollars during their years of operation. By 1906, it was decided that in light of the gold rich seams surrounding her harbors, Juneau was to be named the capitol of the territory. The central government operations were moved from Sitka and continue to operate out of Juneau to this day, making Juneau the only state capitol in the United States that is not accessible by land, as primary access to the city is by air and sea, and there are no roads connecting the city to the rest of North America.

With the growth of the mining industry and government operations came the inevitable entrepreneurs and businessmen who are typically drawn to wealth. Almost overnight, a slew of hardware stores, restaurants, saloons, hotels, gambling parlors and bordellos lined the hillsides of Juneau and nearby Douglas. Most of these establishments are long since gone, the victims of fires or the progress of civilization. One remains, a treasured landmark to Juneau's rough and tumble mining past, the Alaskan Hotel and Bar.

Considered to be the oldest still operating hotel in the state, the Alaskan Hotel was the brainchild of three unlikely partners. After striking it rich in the Canadian caribou country of Atlin, two brothers, by the names of James and John McCloskey decided they would invest in the future of Alaska by building a hotel near the busy waterfront in the business district of Juneau. At the time, there were many boarding houses and shacks, but few establishments refined enough to attract the gold of the wealthy miners passing through from the gold fields. The McCloskys sought the assistance of an experienced hotelier by the name of Jules B. Caro to help put their riches to good use. Construction began in April 1913 and took about five months.

Opening night was a major event in the territory, with free ferry rides bringing in citizens throughout the night from nearby Douglas Island. Champagne and music flowed well into the early morning hours. The doors officially opened on September 16, 1913 to much fanfare. The three-story, 42-room hotel was fashioned in an ornate, late Victorian "Queen Anne" style. Mixed in with the rugged Alaskan construction, the hotel's image as the finest establishment in town was complemented with large bay windows and stained glass, detailed lattice work, steam heat and lavish interior finishing. But just below the surface of the haughty hotel—hailed as the premiere place to rest one's head in the Alaskan territories—lurked a dark, seedy underbelly. The Alaskan was also well known as a notorious house of prostitution.

It is most likely in this capacity that the numerous reports of paranormal activity in the building begin. The majority of ghost sightings in the hotel involve the spirit of a young woman the staff has named Alice. The story goes that Alice was the newlywed wife of one of the many miners attracted to the area with the promise of unbounded wealth. The couple checked into the Alaskan and the husband set out to find a suitable claim. After a while, he realized that the trip was foolish. Nothing worthwhile was left to claim in the immediate vicinity and hadn't been available for years. At the protests of Alice, the stubborn man headed off to scout some territory far into the mountains, promising to be back within three weeks. Alice waited patiently as the weeks ticked by, but after the third week, there was no sign of her beloved. Days stretched to weeks and weeks into months, but still there was no sign of him. What was she to do? Her money eventually ran out, and Alice began accumulating a sizable debt to the hoteliers by continuing to occupy her room. Sadly, believing her husband to be dead and too broke to afford a ticket home, she was left with little other choice but to work in the hotel. Her youth and beauty did not go unnoticed by the men of the camp, and she was forced into the world's oldest profession in the very room she had waited for her spouse.

Tragically, within just a few weeks of taking up her new occupation, her husband miraculously returned to town. Rushing up the stairs to embrace his wife he was stopped and informed of her new profession. Horrified to find what she had been up to while he was away, the man stormed into their former love nest to confront her. An argument ensued and things got out of hand. The man disappeared into the night, never to be seen again and leaving the cold, lifeless body of Alice in the room where she'd lost everything she ever had.

In the years since Alice's murder, the hotel has become a veritable hotbed for paranormal activity. Much of the phenomena are relegated to the rooms 218 and 219, which are supposedly the rooms nearest to where Alice was murdered. The hotel was remodeled in 1978 and has changed in configuration since its earliest design. Staff and guests report feeling very uncomfortable in this section of the hotel, as if someone is watching them. Many claim to feel an overwhelming sense of sadness and dread come over them, out of nowhere. Many guests, who have no idea of the hotel's haunted history, have even requested to be moved out of this section of the hotel due to such feelings and other, more dreadful experiences. There have been numerous reports of guests waking up in the middle of the night to suddenly find a young woman sitting at the foot of their bed, gazing mournfully out the window to the street below. Some have reported that a woman will appear out of thin air in the rooms, stroke their face lovingly, and vanish as suddenly as she appeared. A former housekeeper tells of cleaning the rooms only to return to find the towels and furniture rearranged and scattered about when there is no possibility that anyone could have entered to do so.

The hauntings are not limited to these rooms. Numerous witnesses have also reported seeing Alice on the staircase of the saloon, materializing and vanishing before their very eyes. Many report ghostly figures in historical garb appearing in the mirrors that surround the bar, only to find nobody in the room to match the reflections. Cold spots and icy winds with no obvious source are commonplace. Perhaps the strangest tale, confirmed by several eyewitnesses, involves one of the women's public bathrooms at the inn. A guest or visitor will typically enter the bathroom and be pleasantly surprised at the elegant, dated décor of the room, finished in a lavish but antiquated style. Often, they will comment on it to the bartender or another patron who gives them a knowing look that they too have found themselves in a place that simply does not exist. Upon hearing that such a bathroom cannot be found in the hotel, the patron will insist upon showing the disbeliever and return to the spot to find a fully modern, normal facility where once, they swore, was a space quite different. Not a trace is left of the room they insisted they were just in, save in the words of the next ghostly tale told to the eager masses of visitors who flock to Southeast Alaska.

The Alaskan is and will remain for some time a staple of any Juneau visit. The great live music, authentic Alaskan furnishings and architecture, and cosmopolitan crowd make it a worthwhile stop for any tourist looking to take in a true North Country watering hole. Just be careful when walking the darkened hallways and keep your wits about you when visiting the recesses of this still-vibrant piece of history. The spirits here may not always leave a hangover, but their memory, which lingers much longer, will take more than coffee and aspirin to forget.

The Alaskan Hotel Bar.

Winter and Pond. Photo Collection, courtesy Alaska State Library.

McCabe College, built in 1899, which later served variously as a school, court house, jail, marshal's office, and city hall and museum.

Anna Montgomery Rolston Photo Collection, courtesy Alaska State Library.

The Ghost of McCabe College

Former Skagway Police Officer Alan White has gone on record detailing numerous ghostly experiences he witnessed during his late night shifts at what was once a Methodist preparatory school.

Little attention has been paid to the stories of the children of the Alaskan frontier. One need only to head to the nearest Alaskan bookstore to see shelves filled with accounts of the tribes whose histories go back thousands of years, to the intrepid men who traveled into unknown lands in search of material wealth, to the women who accompanied them and often carved their own destiny out of the snows. Even the beasts of burden who toiled for their masters have been given attention through the works of storytellers and poets like Jack London and Robert Service. But other than a few, sparse academic works, almost no attention has been paid to the children who accompanied them.

It is noteworthy that the oldest human remains found in Alaska to date are those of a child. In 2011, researchers discovered the twenty percent intact skeleton of a three year old that was cremated and buried in the Tanana River Valley 11,500 years ago. One cannot help but wonder what this child's early life was like.

Was there constant danger for such a young soul? When would the child have been expected to perform duties to benefit his or her family? What invaluable lessons were learned in his or her short time on this earth?

Knowledge is as precious a tool in Alaska as fire, shelter or weaponry. From an early age, indigenous children were taught a variety of complex and necessary skills: which plants were edible and which cured sicknesses? Where could one find the best material for making tools? How could one efficiently build the implements needed for survival? This wisdom not only allowed a child to survive day-to-day life in the wilderness, it also ensured the survival of future clan members, as it was passed down from generation to generation. Even today, such knowledge continues to be passed on to the youth in Native communities and elsewhere—an unbroken cultural legacy going back to the time of the mastodon. While in some cases this knowledge is no longer essential for survival, many elders today look upon these teachings as a direct link to the collective past of their people.

The arrival of the Russians across the Bering Sea brought western education to the people of Alaska, supplementing their lessons by the campfire with those in the classroom. Instructors provided by the Russian-American Company and the Russian Orthodox Church formed schools in Southeast Alaska and the Aleutian Island region to promote literacy for Native children. It was believed that such programs would encourage the Native communities to adopt Russian Orthodox religion and therefore be more open to assimilation into the Russian way of life and commerce. The programs proved quite successful, particularly in the Aleutians. Many Aleutic and Yupik villages soon produced prolific readers and writers of both the Russian and Aleutic languages.

On May 17, 1884, almost two decades after Alaska became a sovereign territory of the United States, the U.S. government passed what was known as the First Organic Act. In essence, the Organic Act provided a rough form of government in the territory of Alaska. A territorial governor based in Sitka would be responsible for the establishment of courts, law enforcement, commissioners and a federally funded school system. At the time, indigenous peoples still occupied the majority in inhabited Alaska, with some census records indicating the presence of only 430 non-military whites to the more than 33,000 Natives. Given the ratio, it can be surmised that such educational measures were provided predominantly for the indigenous people's educational welfare, though education was provided regardless of race. Four years later, Alaskan educational programs were placed under the jurisdiction of the Bureau of Education, a subsidiary of the Department of the Interior.

Just prior to the beginning of the Klondike Gold Rush, a system of schools were set up throughout existing Alaskan villages. The predominantly Native and Russian-American students were held to a strictly enforced English-only curriculum that taught American history and citizenship, English, Mathematics, and practical industrial skills in mining, logging and fishing, but often disregarding many traditional Native customs and teachings. While most of the schools were funded and operated directly by the federal government, a new wave of Christian missionaries also began receiving federal contracts to teach throughout Alaska. It is in just such a Christian-founded school that several strange and unexplained events occurred. Though the school bell no longer rings in Skagway's McCabe College, a police officer by the name of Alan White received an important lesson in the things that go bump in the night that no science class can explain.

But, first, the story begins with the construction of the school. The arrival of tens of thousands of miners to the northern reaches of Southeast Alaska brought new life to what were then sparsely occupied valleys. In the mad dash to get north to the gold fields of Dawson, time was precious and little of it was spent on the infrastructure of the boomtowns. Other than creating grids to establish lots sold off to businessmen looking to fleece the miners passing through, few of the swelling communities took on any civic improvements. Though most of the arrivals to these towns were single men with little or no interest in remaining around for long, some entrepreneurs and their families decided the real riches could be found in towns like Dyea, Haines and Skagway. Upon arrival to these muddy mining camps, the families realized their children had little or no formal education opportunities. To keep them off the streets and to put money into the family coffer, the children were often forced to take jobs in the town as newsboys, cooks assistants or general laborers. The work was often difficult, and the hours were often long. Even if there had been child labor laws at the time, the territory of Alaska was far too distant for such laws to have been enforced.

Particularly removed from most law during these first days of the Klondike Gold Rush was the town of Skagway. There at the terminus of the Pacific Ocean, the last stop of the Inside Passage, 10,000 year-round residents plied their wares and performed their services for the thousands of miners passing through on their climb up the White Pass and into the interior. Thankfully, this gateway to the Klondike soon acquired aspirations for permanence and respectability and took measures toward childhood education. By October of 1898, a small schoolhouse was constructed under the Organic Act in order to provide the children with a basic education and a means to escape the toils of everyday working life. Because of limited resources, however, the education provided initially only offered Kindergarten through eighth grade. Beyond that point, the children were to be educated in the home or in the streets or mountains that surrounded Skagway. This situation did not sit well with a new arrival to Skagway by the name of Rev. James Walter.

A Methodist minister by trade, Walter brought his two young daughters with him to Skagway and was disturbed by the lack college preparatory education. He envisioned this prosperous city by the sea as one with limitless potential for growth, but fully realized that with only an eighth grade education, her citizenry would never realize their full potential. He immediately set out to start an institution with the aim of providing advanced education to prepare Skagway's youth for studies at university. On May 6, 1899, ground was broken on what became known as McCabe College. The school's namesake, Bishop Charles McCabe, was a well-respected proponent of university education and a Civil War prison camp survivor.

The building was a very impressive architectural feat, and it remains so to this day. Its three stories are made of local timber and granite brought south via the White Pass and Yukon Railroad. Gothic in appearance, McCabe College stands over most of the structures in town, and is today only overshadowed by the towering cruise ships that dock there five months out of the year. By early 1900, the structure was complete—an imposing and permanent mark of progress in what had once been a lawless boom town. The preparatory school provided a standard classical education with a focus on mathematics, natural science, Latin, Greek and modern language instruction. It was headed by Reverend Lamont Gordon, an Oxford-educated instructor. In the first term of operation, the school boasted fifty students who paid $16.70 per fourteen-week term or $5.50 per month.

Sadly, the prosperity and progress Skagway enjoyed would soon be over. New gold strikes further away from the White Pass route and a decline in production at the mines in Dawson led to a collapse in the local population. Unable to support the university any longer, the Methodist church closed the doors of McCabe College in December 1900 and sold the granite building that housed it to the United States government. For years, it was used as the U.S. courthouse, marshal's office, commissioner's office and city jail. It is perhaps in its jail capacity that the story of its haunting begins.

Many court cases, some of which involved death sentences, were heard in the building. Many accused criminals spent countless hours locked inside the granite walls awaiting their fate. Adjacent to the railroad tracks, one can almost imagine the free floating sounds of whistling trains headed north over the mountains and on toward untamed lands, ringing in the ears of the guilty and the innocent alike, some doomed to never step foot on free soil again. Such torments would be almost unbearable. To make matters worse, the cold chill of winter would seep through the walls, leaving their hearts locked in icy remorse amid what was once a land of promise and possibility. One shudders to think of the sorrows felt and the misdeeds spoken of in this seemingly quaint and stoic structure. For over fifty years, the U.S. government held court and prisoners alike within the confines of old McCabe College. But, by 1956, even these duties had become irregular in the shrinking town of Skagway and the building was sold to the city. It was then converted it into City Hall, a police station and a museum recalling Skagway's early history. It is in this form that Officer Alan. B. White encountered something beyond the laws of the living.

Officer White has spoken of this ghostly tale on several occasions, but most notably on the October 29, 2011 radio talk show Coast to Coast AM, a well-known and popular evening program that discusses ghosts and other unexplained paranormal phenomena. Ever since he was a young man, White had always wanted to explore Alaska. Being a young graduate recently out of the police academy, he figured the timing was perfect to fulfill his lifelong dream. At the time, there were 23 law enforcement offices throughout the entire state of Alaska. White applied to all of them, but the only one to offer White employment was Skagway.

Upon his arrival, he was assigned the graveyard shift and reported for duty in McCabe College. He was immediately overcome by the grand architecture of the structure and the beauty and stillness of the land that surrounded the little town. During his first few shifts, alone at the desk in the old college, he began hearing the creaks and groans typical of an older building settling in a windy place such as Skagway, so he brushed them off as nothing more than what was to be expected. Life was good there, and the eight hundred people who lived in town did not require much policing in the wee hours of the morning. That was not always so. Stories of the building's history as a jail and accounts of the horrible atrocities committed in the name of greed and passion abound in Skagway, and White was right in the heart of it all.

One very late night, while working on a report at his desk, White heard a door loudly creak shut. The telltale groan and slam of the door was immediately recognizable, as he had heard it many times before. Down the hallway was the police storage room. The room had once served as a jail cell, and was protected by an extremely heavy, old oaken door that was over two inches thick. It would not stay open on its own, and whenever it would shut, it would emit the noise he heard. He walked down the unlit hall toward the door and found it closed. He initially assumed it must have been propped open and the wind from an open window blew it shut. However, upon examination he found no open windows and nothing that could have propped the heavy door open. He looked around the office and, finding nothing out of place, he made sure the door was securely shut and returned to his desk. To his surprise, after a few minutes, he again heard the unmistakable sound of the heavy door screeching shut.

Officer White immediately sprang to attention. This was no joke, and there was no doubt someone illegally entered the building. The museum upstairs was full of priceless gold rush artifacts, and the storage room was full of the officers' equipment. Both areas could be robbed and net a hefty profit on the black market, but nobody was about to take anything on White's watch. He drew his weapon and stalked down the hallway toward the storage room the culprit entered. The darkness and shadows played tricks on his mind as he approached the solid oaken door. He flung open the door, gun drawn, and turned on the light to confront the burglar. Not a soul was in the room. Indeed, not a soul was to be found anywhere on the first floor. A chill ran through White's body as he searched the immediate area. There is no way someone would have been able to get in or out of the storage room without White hearing their footsteps on the creaky, wooden floor. Alarmed and in disbelief, White again approached the old wooden door, made sure it was securely shut and tested it several times to ensure it would not be possible to open on its own. He returned to his desk, and before he had the chance to settle in again the unmistakable sound of the door rung through the police headquarters. Now terrified, he ran to the door and just what he feared came true. There was nobody there. The door was securely shut to the point that it was difficult to open. No other door within McCabe College was capable of making such a noise. He was alone.

White returned to the desk, practically shivering in terror when the door slammed shut again. No longer willing to play this unseen specters game, he remained at his desk and continued to work. Then, out of nowhere, White heard the unmistakable sound of footsteps loudly tromping around in the museum above him. The steps were rhythmic, pacing back and forth, back and forth in a measured cadence. At the same time, he once again heard the heavy wooden door open, and then the unmistakable sound of something crashing and banging in the storage room. He again ran to the room, gun drawn, only to find nothing out of place, and nobody inside. Scared and a little angry that his dream job in his dream location came with such an unexpected price, White yelled out to the seemingly empty building, "Is that the best you can do? You walk around a room and crash into something?"

It did not take long for an answer. Again, as soon as he sat down, the door slammed shut again. This happened several more times through the night, but White did his best to ignore it. He decided to keep the story to himself, lest he be ridiculed and potentially ruled unfit for duty. In the following weeks, strange things would occasionally happen on his night shift. Before long, the incident occurred again. It was the same pattern. The door would open and shut by itself, and then he would hear measured, rhythmic pacing directly above the police office. White kept the tales of ghostly activities to himself, but as soon as the opportunity to transfer to an earlier shift was offered, he happily took it.

White befriended the new late shift officer and casually asked if the man ever heard anything weird during his shift. It was of little surprise to White that the officer confided in him that he indeed had, and then went on to describe the same exact phenomena White experienced. The new officer was quite shaken up by the noises. He had come to Alaska to police the living, not the dead. He had never even considered the possibility that ghosts might be real, prior to his late-night shift at McCabe College, but now he was certain there was something beyond the grave.

What did these trusted police officers both hear independently of each other? Is it possible that a convicted murderer is recreating his last walk toward his death? Is the rhythmic pacing heard upstairs the footsteps of a long since gone lawyer pleading a case in court he could never fully resolve? Is it instead the steps of a dedicated teacher forever instructing a long since passed Skagway youth? What of the crashing noise? Is it the sound of a body thundering into the afterworld with the aid of a noose and gallows? Those that could tell us do not seem interested in contact. Rather, it seems to be their goal to terrify in the dark from the shadows, and forever remain things that go bump in the night.

Ghosts at the Fraternal Order of the Eagles #25 Hall

The Fraternal Order of the Eagles Lodge #25 is built from two Gold Rush Era hotels and a World War II barracks. Stories of poltergeist activity abound in all three places, and the restless dead continue to walk the halls they frequented in life.

It is impossible to survive in the rugged cities and encampments of the Last Frontier without the helping hand of others. If standing alone against the harsh elements and foreboding dangers this country hurls toward you, the chances are better than not that a grave awaits your presence. The trees cut to manufacture lumber for shelter and transportation cannot be easily moved alone. The killing and preparation of fish and game can be done significantly more expediently with a trusted friend or two at your side, working as a team to secure foodstuffs for the winter. An injury that can render a man helpless can be overcome by the goodness and charity of one's fellow man. But far worse to most than physical injury are the eight-month winters of the north and the long darkness they bring. Such factors have the power to depress even the most stalwart of loners. A few winters spent alone can be as certain a death sentence as the embrace of a grizzly bear. Companionship in Southeast Alaska is no frivolous luxury—it is a necessity.

Archaeological evidence indicates that ever since the arrival of mankind to Alaska some 10,000 years ago, most humans lived at least part of the year in large group settings. The abundance of resources in the summer allowed for large-scale fishing and hunting encampments, often near major rivers. Such camps afforded cooperation among families, sharing their burdens in procuring resources for winter. The remnants of their semi-subterranean pit houses and wooden long houses indicate these people lived in villages, many of which were capable of supporting hundreds or even thousands of people. In the long winter, those same tribes would often separate into smaller groups, hunkering down into an indoor and sedentary life. It was a time to warm their bodies by the family hearth, occupying their days and nights with ancient tale-telling, crafting art and useful tools, eating from their winter stores and teaching the young ones the traditions of their people.

The white men who came up to Alaska following riches and freedom were not so different from those who came before them. Those who poured into the region soon found that the lifestyles and habits of these ancient Native peoples were well adapted to the harsh conditions they faced. Rather than the "every man for himself" mantra that ruled the trails to Dawson City, the attitude in Southeast Alaska towns included camaraderie and brotherhood that allowed residents to accomplish tasks more easily in the harsh environment of the Final Frontier. Of course, long before the call for gold led men by the thousands up the Inside Passage, the concept of a fraternal organization was alive and well.

Whether collegiate or adult in their composition, fraternal organizations typically encouraged various civic virtues such as brotherhood, charity, and leadership. Perhaps the most famous of such societies is the Freemasons. Allegedly begun from organized guilds of stonemasons in order to control qualification standards and clientele acquisition, Freemasonry as it is known today has been in existence since at least the late 1500s and possibly as early as 1425. The fraternity eventually moved out of Europe with the arrival of Scottish immigrants in the Americas. Many of the founding fathers of the United States are counted in their membership. The push to new frontiers did not end there for the Masons. They made the trek all the way up to Alaska, and a lodge in Skagway was organized and approved on November 30, 1900.

Skagway was home to several such fraternal organizations during the gold rush, and some are still in existence today. These days, when driving down the main thoroughfare of Skagway one cannot miss the hall of the Arctic Brotherhood. Constructed in 1899, the building's front façade is made up of more than 8,800 pieces of driftwood collected from the tidal flats by initiates and arranged in elaborate patterns. The order was founded on February 26, 1899, by friends well accustomed to life in the north, while on board a ship bound for the port city of Skagway. They sought to create a fraternal order specifically for those enduring the harsh way of Alaskan life. The men wanted a band of brothers capable of truly coming to one another's aid in the inevitable times of need. It proved to be a great success. Within several months the eleven founders had grown to a brotherhood of three hundred. At its height, the membership rolls counted 10,000 men in 32 lodges spread out across Alaska and Canada. Unfortunately, within thirty years the lodge's numbers had been reduced significantly by the succession of gold rushes in the north, and the proud traditions of the Arctic Brotherhood fell into the annals of history.

Another major lodge during the gold rush that still exists in Skagway today is the Benevolent and Protective Order of the Elks: Lodge No. 431. It began in Skagway at the height of the stampede to the north on October 12, 1898. The first meeting of the lodge boasted participation from much of the civic and business players in town. Originally held in Keelar's Opera House, whose proprietor Frank Keeler was the first Exalted Ruler, the Elks began construction on a permanent lodge once located just east of Broadway on 6th Avenue. Unfortunately, the building burned in 1904 but was subsequently rebuilt in a grand and opulent style seldom seen after the gold rush. The lodge maintained a roll call of several hundred members, no small feat for a town whose population had dwindled to less than 1,000. Sadly, on November 7, 1942, the lodge again caught fire and was burned to the ground. This time the culprit was a group of men in the United States Army who left an unattended stove that spread into an uncontrollable inferno. The Elks levied an official complaint and the Lodge was again relocated, this time to an existing Army bakery on 6th Avenue and State Street, where it remains to this day. The lodge currently boasts more than three hundred active members.

There is one more fraternal order in Skagway still in existence today. Its hall is the oldest clubhouse still used for meetings. It also boasts a historically inspired stage show in the northern wing of its lodge, continuously operated for the tourists and citizens of Skagway for an estimated 91 years. That is not all that this relic of a bygone era boasts. You see, the Fraternal Order of the Eagles Aerie 25's hall also has the distinction of being the most haunted of Skagway's fraternal lodges. Long after the songs and stories of old are sung, long after the happy crowds have returned to their ships, and long after the last drink is imbibed, it appears something remains. A restless spirit, a forgotten and nameless soul who is no longer counted among the living, walks the very halls that were perhaps once its home.

Six men sitting on a pile of lumber founded the Fraternal Order of the Eagles in 1898. The group meeting on a Seattle wharf that day was made up of theater owners, mulling over what to do regarding a recent musician strike that crippled their business. Though they were able to come up with a plan that day, the men realized that having such meetings regularly was a wonderful idea. Not only was such a meeting an effective way to resolve mutual problems, but they discovered they genuinely enjoyed drinking heavily and carousing together. With a clink of the glasses and a toast to the future, the lodge was born. There and then they decided to found a loosely organized fraternal organization, initially known as the "Order of Good Things." The first lodges were the stages of their six respective theaters, and membership quickly boomed. Before long, a stuffed eagle had become their official mascot, and within a few months, the group had changed their name to the Fraternal Order of the Eagles, honoring their feathered totem. Given the fact that theater owners began the order, many of the initial memberships were given to members of touring acting troupes. The transient nature of these wandering thespians quickly led to the spreading of the order across much of the western United States. By the time the F.O.E had made its way up to Skagway on June 11, 1899, the Eagles already had 24 lodges in place.

Skagway was an ideal 25th lodge. Much of the initial membership of the lodge, or Aerie, was made up of successful businessmen and civic figureheads of the town, as evidenced by the still existing roll calls. By 1902, the Aerie was holding its meetings just off the southeast corner of 6th Avenue and Broadway Street in the remnants of a gold rush hotel known as the Pacific. The Pacific was initially located on 5th Avenue near Main Street, and photographic evidence suggests that the hotel was where the Aerie met even prior to its relocation onto 6th and Broadway. The structure was multi-storied, and featured a bar and lounge in the lobby. By 1916, the town had changed dramatically from its gold rush heyday., The population had centered its commercial activities on Broadway, putting the Eagles Hall right in the thick of the hustle and bustle of small town life. Kitty corner to the hall, on the northwest corner of 6th and Broadway, a new Bank of Alaska building was set to go up. Like the rest of the downtown area, the lot planned for the bank was already occupied and needed to be cleared for the project. It was not just any building that was set for removal; it was another well-known hotel from the gold rush era by the name of the Mondamin. Not wanting to let go of the valuable and historically pertinent structure and needing additional space anyway, the Eagles moved the Mondamin just across the street and incorporated it into the layout of the Aerie.

The Mondamin is now perhaps best known as the home of the infamous outlaw Jefferson Randolph Smith, or "Soapy" as he is most commonly known. The official log of the Mondamin clearly shows his signature signed into room six. Correspondence in the possession of the descendants of Jeff Smith are all addressed from this room throughout his tumultuous tenure in Skagway until his death, indicating that this was most likely his permanent residence in town. Room six would have been on the second floor in the northwest portion of the building. Such a position afforded a bird's eye view of Jeff. Smith's Parlor, the nefarious nerve center of his criminal operations in Skagway. Sometime following World War II, a military barracks was added onto the lodge, making F.O.E. Aerie #25 three historical buildings all in one.

Today, if you happen to be a member of the F.O.E. or accompany one, you can sit right in the old bar room of the Pacific and enjoy the same spirits that have been poured here for over 110 years. If drinking is not your game, then just through a set of ancient wooden doors, in what was once the Mondamin, you can grab a bag of popcorn and take in a show that has become a time honored tradition in the gateway to the Klondike, the famous Days of '98 show. The structure of the northern portion of the Mondamin has been hollowed out and transformed into a gorgeous theater where several times a day, rain or shine, performers from around the world gather seasonally to recreate the scenes and spectacles of the heyday of Skagway in the last great gold rush of the American frontier.

In some form or another, the Days of '98 show has been around for over 91 years. Today, the show revolves around the life and times of Soapy Smith, who happened to live just offstage in the northwest corner of the structure. The first evidence of some form of the Days of '98 show comes to us from a letter brought to the attention of Jonathan Baldwin, the current owner and a performer at the show. The letter, written in 1923, was given to him by the great granddaughter of a woman that had come to Skagway that year to teach elementary school. In the letter, she speaks enthusiastically of a function she was attending at the White Pass Athletic Club to "celebrate the days of '98". The letter details that she enjoyed the gambling where she won $5,000 of Soapy's fake money, Cancan dancing and especially the bottle of bathtub Gin that a mysterious scoundrel named Bill had managed to acquire.

By 1925, the Eagles Auxiliary, an all-female branch of the Aerie, began operating a show featuring Cancan dancing and mock gambling as a Christmas fundraiser. The occasional cruise ship was also treated to performances, and the show eventually evolved into a full blown tourist extravaganza whenever visitors were in port. By the 1970s, another show—this one focusing specifically on the life and times of Soapy Smith—was performing regularly for tourists at the hall of the Arctic Brotherhood. By 1978, the proprietors Tom Biss and Jim Richards chose to combine the shows, incorporating a recreation of Smith's famous soap pitch, Cancan dancing, mock gambling, and selected readings of Robert Service poetry. From then until today, the celebrated Days of '98 show has thrilled audiences from all over the world, giving them a taste of frontier life in the heyday of a gold rush boom town. But long after the applause has died out, the laughter has ceased and the old edifice closes up for the night, something remains behind.

Stories of restless spirits and phantom noises abound in the hall, particularly in the remnants of the old Mondamin Hotel.

The majority of paranormal activity within the Eagles hall seems to be centered on the second floor of the old Mondamin Hotel. Historically, this would have been where the bulk of the guest rooms were located, including that of Soapy Smith. In fact, there is one particular spot in the theater that appears to be the epicenter of paranormal activity, which according to owner Jon Baldwin, was once the location of Soapy's old room. Unfortunately, it is impossible to enter room six—Soapy's Skagway domicile—as it no longer exists. Alterations made for the current theater led to the removal of large sections of the second floor of the old Mondamin. Howvever, the renovations do not appear to have deterred former residents from occupying their old rooms. Actors have long complained of strange cold spots coming from the northwest corner of the theater, just below where Soapy lived. Without warning, doors in the theater will slam shut, often followed by ghostly footsteps without a source. Light switches will turn on by themselves when nobody is in the building other than the terrified observer of the strange phenomena.

Not all of the second floor of the Mondamin was removed in construction of the theater. The L-shaped structure's other half has been converted into office space for club operations and meetings. Many Eagles members, working late into the night in the offices, have heard a brother come up the staircase and walk toward them across the ancient floor and approach the door. Turning to greet them, they discover they are completely alone.

Nobody knows for sure what haunts the old Mondamin today. There are, however, two possible explanations. The first is that Soapy, Skagway's outlaw martyr, continues to occupy the remnants of room six and the surrounding area. It is not implausible that a man who came to such a desperate end could still remain. A second, and significantly more mysterious story comes to us from Jon Baldwin.

While researching the story of the actors and actresses that worked and lived in Skagway during the gold rush, Jon came upon the tale of a young couple that 1900 census records indicate lived in the Mondamin Hotel. The story goes that the man and woman fell deeply in love during their time in Skagway, and were inseparable upon her muddy streets and dingy bedrooms. However, as passionate romances often go, the fire began to fade. Eventually, the gold rush stampede that gave birth to Skagway dwindled and the troupe the couple belonged to moved up to Dawson.

It was here that the trouble truly began. The woman became increasingly displeased with her lover, and eventually the man noticed her affections shifting to a successful miner from the camp. Enraged and drunken, he confronted his lover, who confessed she had fallen out of love with him and was planning to run away with the wealthy miner. Heartbroken and livid with loss, the man drew his pistol and shot her dead, taking his own life immediately after. It is speculated that both spirits returned to the place where they were once happy, their lovers' nest inside what is now the nest of Skagway Eagles Aerie #25.

Unfortunately, the gold rush was a tumultuous time and records for much of the triumph and tragedy experienced on the trail of '98 are lost or unavailable. The story of this couple, at the time of publication, remains just that—a story. Are the ghosts that haunt the Eagles' Lodge the souls of Soapy Smith or the long dead lovers? Are they, perhaps, the ghosts of those whose stories have long been forgotten? Death was a commonplace occurrence during the heyday of the gold rush, and not all who were lost are remembered. Shallow depressions and weathered bones all over Skagway and its neighboring town of Dyea attest to the cruelty and indifference of time and memory, and perhaps those who walk the halls of the lodge simply yearn for recognition. The only entity who knows for sure, has thus far not said a word.

The Silverbow Inn and Bakery

The historic bakery is said to be haunted by the ghost of its founder, a German immigrant named Gus Messerschmidt.

Not all ghost stories begin with horrific accidents or brutal murders. Not all ghost stories end with terror and mournful phantoms forever doomed to walk the site of their untimely end. Sometimes, it appears that a spirit remains out of love for a particular location. Sometimes, a soul's dedication to a particular duty cherished in life extends into death. Such is the case of the ghost of the Silverbow Inn and Bakery.

The Silverbow has the distinction of being the oldest continuously operating bakery in Alaska. Located in the heart of downtown Juneau, just a few blocks away from the icy depths of the Pacific, the bakery has, in one form or another, catered to the waterfront throngs of miners, citizens and tourists since 1899. The original owner of the property was known as Gus Messerschmidt. Born in Germany in 1872 as Gustav Henry Messerschmidt, he moved to the United States in 1887 in search of a better life. He quickly grew tired of the lack of opportunities in the East for a newly arrived immigrant with little money and decided to head for the West. Messerschmidt sailed a freighter around Cape Horn to San Francisco, where his sister lived. It was there that Gus found his true calling as a baker while working in a shop downtown and fine-tuning his skills.

Finding the trade suited his precise and congenial nature, but thirsting for adventure and a chance to make something of himself on unproven ground, Messerschmidt set out to the boom town of Placerville, California, and opened his own shop. Like most successful boomtown businesses, the money was only around for as long as the miners were, but Gus found himself drawn to the sense of adventure and limitless financial possibilities of mining towns. Soon the gold in Placerville panned out, and he went further north to the town of Tacoma, Washington. Not long after his move, news of gold in the Klondike hit the world like a thunderbolt. Gus had to be a part of it. Bakery owner Ernst Beihl hired him as a baker in Juneau. Like many of those who became well off from the Klondike Gold Rush, it was not in the creeks and mountains and mines that Beihl and Messerschmidt looked for their fortunes, but in the town where the hard working prospectors would come to spend their pokes.

Messerschmidt arrived in Juneau, an important stop on the way to the Klondike, in November of 1898 aboard the steamer *Cottage City*. For unspecified reasons, but likely due to a desire to run his own business, Gus parted ways with Beihl and opened his own bakery in May of 1899. Messerschmidt's San Francisco Bakery was located on Main Street, and it was an immediate success. One can imagine the miners, who have been away from the creature comforts of home and civilization for months or even years, salivating at the smells of his fresh baked delicacies as they disembarked ships and made their way into the port town. The sirens' song of fresh baked apple strudel, pies, cakes and homemade bread would have been worth whatever Messerschmidt asked. The bakery became a must-stop for all who passed through.

It was not only in Juneau's business community that he found success. In late June of 1899, Gertrude Rosina Hermle, a friend of his sister, came to Juneau to work as a clerk in his shop. They soon fell in love, and were married on September 21, 1899. Soon after, the couple moved into an apartment together above the bakery. By 1900, they moved their successful business to its second location on Seward Street. The building that housed the San Francisco Bakery there was a small frame structure. It was in the bakery's upstairs apartment that several of their nine children were born.

As is typical with frontier towns, buildings were much more permanent than their locations. New opportunities for better lots closer to the hustle and bustle were constant. Shop keepers sold their lots quickly at the news of a new strike in some distant land, deeds were lost in high stakes card games, and owners sometimes up and left for the comforts of their faraway homes. As the throngs of prospectors coming through Juneau began to wane, Messerschmidt decided to stop his wandering. He purchased the lot where the Silverbow Bakery and Inn sits today from Louie LaPointe in 1902 and brought his already-built wooden structure to the newly acquired land. By 1914 Gus added a three-story concrete building to his original shop that allowed for additional kitchen space and several more apartments. The life of the Messerschmidts followed a well-ordered routine of rising early to make the days' baked goods and keeping the shop open until they were all sold. They continued to live above the store in the wooden building. Gus saw his dreams of family and fortunes thrive in their harbor home.

The patriarch of Alaska's Messerschmidt clan passed away in 1938, but rumors persist that something of him lives on. Besides his numerous descendants who still live in Alaska, many customers, employees and guests of The Silverbow claim the spirit of this man still walks the halls of his beloved home and business in the early hours of the morning, making sure everything is ready for the day ahead.

The stories began with the purchase of the property in 1977 by husband and wife Ken Alper and Jill Ramiel. After a three-month remodeling process, the couple's familiar dream of making it in the Last Frontier came to fruition. In no time, their delicious bagels became a staple in the diets of many a Juneau resident, and the location provided an excellent gathering place for those who lived and worked in the business district. Like the Messerschmidts, the couple chose to live upstairs, therefore living and working in the same environment as their predecessors. Before long, tales of strange sounds, poltergeist activity and phantom apparitions were passed on to the new owners. Were they just stories or, could it be that they were not alone in the business of their dreams?

In due time, it became apparent that the location, indeed, was not theirs alone. According to an October 2013 interview in the *Capital City Weekly*, Alper was quoted as saying, "In the kitchen in particular with the bakers, things would move suddenly, carts would roll across the floor, a sound would come through the ceiling," Alper said. "It was never anything hostile—things along those lines."

The activity seemed to be confined to the early morning hours, and was focused solely on those preparing the bakery for the day. Many speculated that the unexplained phenomena were the result of old Gus Messerschmidt himself, watching over his beloved business to make sure it was still in working order. It became so commonplace to have a pan crash with no warning to the floor or a necessary utensil go missing that the staff would laugh about it to one another. But the laughter stopped, and rumors of who was behind the phenomena were confirmed when a baker, who was also living at the business, woke up early one morning and looked in the mirror. Rubbing sleepy eyes and coming to in the haze of a Juneau morning, he was shocked by the image in the mirror. Directly behind the baker was the visage of the former owner, long since dead, staring back at him.

In 2000, the Silverbow acquired a new dishwasher of Inupiaq descent who had just arrived in Juneau. The man immediately felt uneasy in the property and before long asked Alper if he was aware of any spirits on the property. Shocked, Alper informed him of the stories and the unexplained happenings. The Inupiaq man was not surprised and confided in Alper that he was not comfortable working in the building alone at night. The man asked if he could perform a ceremony to free the spirit, as it was trapped to its obligations on earth and needed to be shown rest. Alper acquiesced, and the man carried out a traditional Inupaiq exorcism.

According to the couple, the sightings largely seemed to go away. Just like their predecessors, Alper, Ramiel and their growing family have become indispensable to the Juneau Community. At the time of publication, Alper serves as the director of the State of Alaska's Department of Revenue. The business has grown to include a hotel/bed and breakfast, a wine bar, and a modern and relaxing environment to enjoy a delicious bagel or a glass of wine away from the crowds that return to the port town each summer. Unfortunately, despite the exorcism, guests at the hotel still comment about strange sounds, moving objects and phantom apparitions. But those visiting should not fear, for Gus Messerschmidt appears to be merely concerned about the daily running of his business and would never dream of having customers leave his bakery with a bad taste in their mouths.

The Spirit of Sawmill Creek Road

Local legend tells of a woman killed in a horrific accident, now doomed forever to walk the road where she died.

Like most drives in Alaska, Sawmill Creek Road in Sitka greets the traveler with constant beauty and wonder. Stretching mainly along the south-facing coast as it meanders around Sitka Sound, the route is a varied tapestry of daily life and beauty through the city.

The road begins in earnest in the bustling downtown district and goes east to pass a series of quaint homes, small businesses bustling with activity and, of course, it travels right along the splendor of the surrounding wilderness and ocean. A lucky few passing by at the right time can even see pods of orca in the distance, hunting for their meals and exploring the deep waters of the sound. But all of this beauty comes with a price.

Sawmill Creek Road, like many older Alaskan routes, was in many places carved out of the granite bedrock and often follows the irregular curvature of the shore. Because of this, the road winds precariously around several blind corners. In the winter, the humidity coming off the ocean freezes on the asphalt, creating the unseen killer that is black ice. Looking away from the road for just a moment has been a death sentence to more than a few weary drivers or those unlucky enough to be in their paths. It is from these unfortunate road conditions and the foolishness of man that a legend has been born. A memory of a horrific accident many years ago that, to this day, echoes in the consciousness of the local population. A woman's death acts as a reminder to the danger ever present for those who get behind a wheel after spending a night at a local watering hole. The reminder given to those who choose to drink and drive is not merely one of law or conscience, but one of gruesome terror and foreboding.

Alaska currently has one of the highest per capita alcohol consumption rates and, according to a Gallup Poll, has twice the national average percentage of residents who are dependent upon alcohol. Many indigenous villages have banned alcohol outright, enforcing said bans with strict fines and imprisonment for introducing drink to the isolated communities. There is no shortage of establishments in Sitka to satisfy the appetite for drink, and most patrons enjoy their local bar without drinking to excess. Some do not heed the warnings posted in every bar about the illegality of intoxication, especially public, in the state of Alaska, and it is in just such a condition that one poor unfortunate soul is forever locked.

As local legend goes, the story begins at what was once known as the Kiksaadi Club. Located just off the Mt. Verstovia trail at the head of Jamestown Bay, the club was certainly not the first structure on the land it sits. It is known that the Russians logged the hillside behind the bar extensively in the 1860s, just prior to turning over all of Russian Alaska to the United States. As it is with many logging and fishing towns like Sitka, after a hard day's work many choose to enjoy a few alcoholic beverages at their local watering hole. Kiksaadi was just such a place. One dark night a woman was drinking to excess in the bar. As per the law, once the bartender discovered her highly intoxicated state he cut her off. The bar was near closing and it was almost time for last call. The woman stumbled out the door and into the night. She passed a large crowd of people in the parking lot readying to head out to an after-hours party in the mountains. Hundreds recall her tripping and stumbling drunkenly toward the road and toward her fate.

She headed in the direction of town, most likely to one of the numerous late night bars in the city center. Unfortunately, she never made it there. The Kiksaadi Club sat on one of the numerous blind corners on the road, and a mass of large bushes and shrubs located right on the corner further impacts visibility. The woman walked toward the bushes and out of sight when all of a sudden the partygoers heard the screeching of tires and a sickening, unmistakable thud of flesh hitting metal. A driver, who was also drunk, had veered off the road and smashed right into the woman. Her body was flung into the bushes, mangled almost beyond recognition. The crowd, knowing immediately what had happened, raced over to the scene of the accident. What occurred next was truly terrible.

The impact had not killed the woman but disfigured her horribly. Her body was broken and writhing. Perhaps because of the numbing agents of drink, perhaps because of the surge of adrenaline following the horrific impact, or perhaps because her spirit desperately clung to the last vestiges of life in her poor body, the woman shot up out of the bushes. Screaming in agony, she stumbled out onto the road, convulsing and crying out for help. Sadly, there was no helping this poor soul. She appeared to be in deep shock and was obviously near death. Perhaps she had no idea what had happened to her. The crowd desperately tried to calm her, but with one foot already in the grave, she paid them no heed. She continued to stumble along the street, screaming and shrieking as her body went into death throws. Finally she collapsed near the bushes where she had been flung into by the impact of the car. An ambulance was called, but before it arrived, the woman took her last breath in this realm and perished on the dangerous corner in front of the Kiksaadi Club.

Following this horrific accident, many reports have come in over the years of a truly disturbing haunting at this corner. Many state they have seen an apparition of a woman from a distance at the blind curve in front of the old bar, weaving in and out of the road, her body disfigured and torn to pieces. When drivers stop to help the woman, she wails a piercing scream before vanishing before their very eyes. Many of those who have seen her admit to being intoxicated at the time of sighting, indicating that perhaps she appears as a warning of the danger such foolish behavior poses to others. There is perhaps a silver lining in the haunting, as many of the intoxicated drivers have pulled over and parked their vehicles for the night after seeing her. Still others report that rather than seeing the apparition herself, they only hear her. The same bushes and shrubs the deceased woman was thrown into remain to this day at the corner, and often people report hearing screams and anguished cries emanating from the bushes and out toward the road.

The Kiksaadi Club is now no more. Not long after the accident, its doors were closed for good. The building has changed ownership several times since the tragic evening that claimed a woman's life, but no business seems to have been able to stick. Most recently, it was known as Rookie's, and was billed as a sports bar. Even that now is no more, and the building has instead been converted into town homes. Residents of the old Kiksaadi Club did not comment on the haunting that takes place along the road in front of their home. But, should you ever find yourself a sheet or two to the wind at a bar in Sitka or anywhere else, do both them and yourself a favor and call a cab. The soul you save just might be your own.

The Gilmore Hotel

The historic Gilmore Hotel of Ketchikan is purported to be haunted by the ghost of its original owner, Patrick Gilmore, as well as the spirit of a woman named Annabelle that may have been a major contributor to the building of the hotel.

Fire is a constant in the north. Whether it serves as a comfort or a calamity, the harbor towns of Southeast Alaska have been shaped by fired since their inception. The first pioneers to arrive on the icy shores of the Pacific shaped their vessels, cooked their meals and warmed their shelters with its power. Often, those very shelters and even whole towns were lost to the powerful element. Ketchikan is no exception. Regularly in recorded history businesses, homes and even whole city blocks have been leveled by devastating fires. Most of these fires were accidental, some were not.

The island community of Ketchikan was established in the early 1880s by Mike Martin. Martin was hired by a group of investors based in Portland, Oregon to investigate the area for use as a salmon cannery and fishery. It was near the present day downtown that he found and claimed the prize he set out for. In 1885, Martin purchased 160 acres located at the mouth of the

Ketchikan River, from Chief Kyan of the Tongass and Cape Fox Tlingit. Seasonally used by the Tlingit people as a fishing camp, the Kitschk-hin or "Thundering Wings of an Eagle" riverfront boasted an extremely dense growth of timber and served as a gateway to the rich salmon waters of the surrounding region. The location proved to serve well.

The first cannery was opened in 1886 and by 1912 four more were built. As miners poured into the region on their way to Dawson City, the town was all too happy to help accommodate the host of newcomers. Ketchikan proved to be an important supply port and stop along the way to the gold fields of the north, leading to further growth on Revillagigedo Island. By the turn of the century, the vast hillside spruce forests that sheltered and warmed the citizenry also led to a boom in the lumber industry. In 1903, the Ketchikan Spruce mill opened, satisfying the need for lumber for construction throughout the region and packing crates for the next seventy years. By 1954, a pulp mill was also built near Ketchikan, which until it closing in 1997, harvested and pulverized millions of dollars of Tongass timber,

Lumber has long been the very lifeblood and bones of Ketchikan. The business district that throngs of tourists walk through today is built on a series of docks and wharves. It has always been in constant danger of fire, as its mostly wooden buildings rest on pilings in the tidal zone and well into the sea. Even the very streets and sidewalks were built of local spruce. Early in Ketchikan's history, the homes and street lamps were lit and heated with wood, coal and oil, burning brightly throughout the long nights and damp days. To make the situation even more dangerous, the town was regularly subjected to high winds whistling down the narrow streets. Fires sprang up regularly. It was up to the citizenry to assemble whatever were resources available to fight them. In June of 1900, a man named D. Smith Harris organized a group of volunteers to serve as a bucket brigade. He encouraged every home to have rain buckets full of water to stop destruction by fire. The volunteers were always at the ready and were expected to be ready regardless of time or weather conditions. Through the years, members of the Ketchikan volunteer fire department would prove to be an asset time and time again—and a scourge, once.

Only a few years after the founding of the volunteer fire department, the call of the Last Frontier was answered by one of her faraway sons. Patrick J. Gilmore arrived in Ketchikan because something inside told him he must. His brother, Peter, had come to Southeast Alaska prior to him, in 1898, to seek his fortune in the gold fields of Dawson. He soon realized the true gold was to be found much further south. In glowing letters sent to their ancestral home of County Galway Ireland, he described to young Pat a land of mountains greener than all of Ireland, rich valleys and waterways full of nature's bounty and beauty beyond compare. Above all, he described in detail a place that gave a chance to anyone with a good work ethic and a keen business sense to make their fortune. The place Peter spoke of was Ketchikan.

It was not long before the power of these letters distracted 22-year-old Patrick from his work on the family farm and he set off on a great adventure. Leaving behind his true love, a teacher named Elizabeth, and all that he knew, he set out for Ketchikan. By the time of his departure, his brother had found success as the proprietor of The Emerald, a popular saloon and boarding house on Front Street that boasted the town's first bowling alley. Finding work as a clothier's apprentice, Patrick settled in well in Ketchikan. He made friends quickly with his easy going ways and dedication to community. By 1905, he opened The Clothing Emporium, a Dock Street outfitter, that sold all the wares necessary for the woodsman and the gentleman in this changing community. With his newfound success in business and his rising status in the community, he felt it was time to bring a little more of his old home to his new. He soon sent for his best friend, Mike Heneghan, who opened a bakery just down the street from "The Clothing Emporium". He also sent for his beloved Lizzie. The two met in Seattle and were married on October 3rd, 1906. Patrick returned to Ketchikan with his bride and built a lovely home on Dunton Street. Within a year they gave birth to their first child, Mary. The Gilmores would go on to have seven children in total, though tragically only four survived to adulthood.

Growing with his young family was also his prominence in the community. He eventually purchased a larger building to accommodate his growing business, renting extra office space in the structure to several medical and therapeutic professionals. In 1910 he began a political career in Alaska, and was elected to the Ketchikan city council for the first of what would prove to be four separate terms. Ever the active participant in his beloved home, he also served on the local school board and was a Democratic delegate to the first Alaska Territorial Convention in Juneau. Everything seemed to be going Gilmore's way. His best friend, Mike Heneghan, even became the first elected mayor in 1916. Gilmore's growing business interests spread into cold storage and banking, necessary for any town and very lucrative. Truly he was a man on the rise.

In February of 1926, opportunity again knocked on Gilmore's door, this time in the form of fire. That month, a large fire downtown quickly grew out of control and destroyed the old Pioneer Hotel as well as nine other buildings in the business district. Earlier in the decade, another mainstay hotel named the Revilla hotel had burned. The destruction of these establishments had left a large gap not only in the bustling business district, but also in the thriving economy of Ketchikan. Patrick Gilmore, ever the eager entrepreneur, was just the man to seize the opportunity. With his attention to detail, and allegedly a good deal of financial support from a well off prostitute named Annabelle who was to run a restaurant in the hotel, work began immediately after the smoke cleared.

Built from the ashes of the fire of 1926, the Gilmore Hotel celebrated its opening day on February 20, 1927, almost a year to the day of the devastating downtown fire. Learning from the misfortunes of his predecessors, Gilmore sought to make his namesake business entirely fireproof. The L-shaped exterior of the hotel was made of concrete, making it resistant to any future fires to which the downtown might succumb. It was also built on a foundation of bedrock, unlike much of the rest of downtown which was built upon pilings in the tidelands. Described at the time as being "...modern in every way," the hotel boasted telephones in each room, modern electric lighting and many private bathrooms. Most importantly, a sprinkler system was put in place in every hall and room within the building. These fireproofing features would prove to be invaluable in the years to come.

The Gilmore Hotel was an immediate success. The first floor was used as a lobby and meeting room and also had room for a tailor shop, Annabelle's restaurant and storefront space. Gilmore remained an active presence in the business throughout his life, but his prominence in the community continued to grow. In 1933, he was elected Mayor of Ketchikan. Much of the town business soon was done inside the concrete confines of the Gilmore. Mayor Gilmore became a fixture of local clubs and community organizations. He was famous for his St. Patrick's Day festivities, proudly wearing his hand tailored green suits and singing Irish folk tunes well into the evening.

Extremely busy during his tenure as mayor, he retired as a clothier. However the Gilmore Hotel proved to be the perfect place to hold court and meet with community leaders and became the seat of his power. In 1944, he reached a personal pinnacle, being appointed U.S. Commissioner and Judge of the Probate Court for the First Judicial District. Tragically, that same year he lost his daughter Elizabeth to pneumonia. Several years later, in 1951, his wife passed away.

Heartbroken and in poor health himself, Judge Gilmore was seen in public less and less. Passersby would often catch a brief glimpse of him through the shop windows of his beloved hotel, late at night, smoking a cigar and pacing the floors, thinking on better times and lost love. Once in a while, he would make an appearance at the Elks Lodge to reminisce of better times over a glass of Irish whiskey. But, the gregarious man about town was broken, worn down by loss and age. By 1953, he was too ill to continue his business, and sold his fireproof building to the Stedman Hotel Company. His son, now a District Attorney in Juneau, moved back to Ketchikan with his wife and daughter to care for Patrick. Despite all of their love and concern, a heartbroken hero of the frontier passed away in February of 1957, thirty years after the opening of his beloved Gilmore Hotel.

At the tail end of Gilmore's rich life, something sinister began brewing in Ketchikan. Rashes of unexplained fires were breaking out downtown. All of them appeared to begin in laundry or utility rooms. All of them appeared to have been started by candles being left near flammable objects. At first it appeared a bizarre coincidence, but soon rumor travelled around the town that the fires were being deliberately set. For a time, the fires were quickly contained by the fire department, and no serious damage was done. This changed on July 15, 1956. All the buildings on Main Street between Mission and Dock were lost in an inferno. Gone were the historic Red Men Lodge, the Ketchikan Meat Company, the local liquor store, the Coliseum Theater and numerous other buildings from Ketchikan's sacred past. All were located just down the street of the Gilmore Hotel. All were gone forever. These fires were purported to begin simultaneously. There was no longer any doubt of it. There was an arsonist in Ketchikan.

Suspects were numerous. Possible motives flew around town like mosquitos in the muskeg. Several other fires attributed to the arsonist were started and quelled in the next few months.

Then, on New Year's Day in 1958 the mad man again struck a fatal blow to the Ketchikan business district. This time, right on Front Street, between Mission and Dock Streets, twelve historic and modern businesses were gutted by fire. Establishments such as the local drugstore, an apartment complex, the Rainbird Café and Bar, Stan's Music Shop and the Alaska Steamship offices were lost forever. Again, all of these were just a stone's throw from the historic and fireproof Gilmore Hotel. On January 25, 1960, near where the Eagle Park is today and just across the street from the Gilmore, fire yet again broke out. This time, the fire destroyed the dockside Hunt Building and several other properties surrounding the Gilmore. Again the fireproof hotel survived the flames. This pattern repeated itself through the year until, mercifully, the likely arsonist was identified.

Volunteer firefighter and Lieutenant Bill Mitchell was the son of the local Ben Franklin store owners. A popular, affable gentleman, the rumors and accusations were a shock to the close-knit community. Mitchell was, like Gilmore before him, an institution in Ketchikan. He served as the President of the Junior Chamber of Commerce. He was acting President of the Jaycees. He managed his parent's store. He was a happily married man. What could bring such a man to do this?

Mitchell was first named officially as a suspect by Al Parkins, a *Ketchikan Daily News* reporter, who noticed that the young lieutenant was always the first to arrive to the scene of every fire. In addition to that, the candles used in the blazes were always a type sold exclusively at his parent's store. Isobel Daigler, the manager of the Coliseum Theater recalled that Mitchell would often stop by and speak to her enthusiastically and excitedly about the fires immediately after they occurred. The police and fire chief were convinced they had their arsonist, but they needed proof. The proof would come in the form of a lie detector test issued to all of the firemen. Unfortunately, when Bill Mitchell's turn came up, he presented excuse after excuse as to why he couldn't make it.

Now convinced they had their man, the polygraph operator and the police and fire chief set up a trap. They released a false story in the newspaper that the operator had headed back to Juneau. Instead, he hid out in the Ingersoll Hotel, not leaving his room for days. Sure enough, Mitchell eventually appeared at the fire house, coming up with a story about a sick relative and profusely apologizing for being absent. When informed that the polygraph operator was in fact in town and ready to test Mitchell, the frightened Lieutenant said that would not be a problem. He would take the polygraph as soon as possible. He just had to first check in on his ailing mother. When he finally did return for the test, he admitted that he was extremely high on phenobarbital. In this condition, any results from the test would be inadmissible in court. The police and fire chiefs decided to indict Mitchell without the polygraph, and a grand jury was put together. After the first hearing, a spooked Mitchell fled Ketchikan for California, where his grandmother lived.

For months, the chaos that had reigned in Ketchikan stopped. Everything returned to normal. People got on with their lives. Then, on the 4th of July, 1961, it happened again. The town was celebrating their freedom in typical style. Streets were blocked off and revelers were crowding local drinking establishments and entertainment booths. At 3:20 p.m., fire was reported in the Tongass Trading Post apartment buildings. The fireman quickly raced to the scene. To their horror, they discovered the building's fire hose had been deliberately cut. Before they could even begin their work to save the building, news of another fire at the Federal Apartments was reported. The team split and began fighting both blazes. A little over an hour later, the Stedman Hotel was reported in flames, directly across the street from the Tongass Trading building. The arsonist had returned. Last year, the suspect would have been obvious. This time there was no Bill Mitchell. He was far away in California with his grandmother. Or was he?

A local policeman, Ray Hackstock, had first noticed a rather large, strange looking woman that was not from town, while directing traffic for the parade. He thought nothing more of it at the time, and like the rest of the men in town fought the three blazes, now convinced his friend Bill was innocent. By that evening, the stories of the woman traveled through town. It was confirmed that just such a large, strange looking woman had been confirmed on the scene of all three fires just before their outbreak. Right around the time the town was putting it all together; a pilot for Ellis Air by the name of Lloyd Tillson reported that he had seen a man dressed as a woman on one of his flights. The woman had boarded a Pan Am flight bound for Seattle. The Seattle FBI was notified, and were waiting for the plane when it landed. Unable to verify the cross dresser's identity, but convinced it was Mitchell, the FBI had no choice but to let her go. She continued onto her final destination of California. It appeared that the suspect would escape unscathed. But, several days later, convinced by his family that it was the right thing to do, Mitchell turned himself in for starting twelve separate fires in Ketchikan. He was picked up by Police Chief Hank Miller in California and flown back to Ketchikan.

Convicted on all counts, Miller was sent to McNeil Island Penitentiary in Washington State. Cooperative and a well behave prisoner, he was eventually paroled and lived out the rest of his days in Fairbanks and California, where he eventually died. His case served as a model for criminal psychologists and his cooperation allowed for the first time an in-depth, scientific look into the mind of a serial arsonist. The motive, it turns out, tied into Mitchell's sexual fantasies and fascination with power and fire. When his wife was asked in court whether or not their sex life could be considered normal, she had responded nervously, "What's normal?"

Pat Gilmore and Bill Mitchell both irrevocably changed

Ketchikan forever, one for the better and one for the worse. Some reports suggest that the numerous hauntings at the Gilmore Hotel may also be a direct result of these men and their actions. The Gilmore is a veritable hot bed of paranormal activity, with stories abounding of everything from poltergeist activity to fully visible apparitions to levitation of guests.

Lela Raymond is the manager of Annabelle's Famous Keg and Chowder House. The restaurant space is the very same that Ketchikan prostitute Annabelle owned and operated in the Gilmore Hotel, paid for with the funds she earned in her former trade. Today, the location is well known for its delicious chowder and welcoming atmosphere. But Lela Raymond and her staff have repeatedly seen and heard things that are all but welcoming. Sights and sounds from beyond this world's realm of understanding.

Raymond has worked at the restaurant in a managerial capacity for the past three years, but also was employed there twenty years earlier. Throughout that time, she has seen and heard of numerous incidents of paranormal activity in the restaurant and within the hotel. One such story began on an otherwise typical morning. Raymond was alone in the restaurant preparing the quiet, empty building for the day's business. She was busy stocking the serving station when all of a sudden, through the mirror in front of her, she saw the unmistakable shadow of a man. The shadow moved across the room, as if the man was walking across the still unopened restaurant. She turned around to inform the intruder that the restaurant would be open shortly. To her dismay, there was nobody there. Spooked, she shook it off and continued with her work. Who was that man? Could it be that the spirit of Mr. Gilmore still paces his hotel, watching over the comings and goings to this very day?

This male spirit is not the only supernatural occurrence in Annabelle's. Several workers have reported seeing Annabelle herself. The situation is always the same. Someone will be working alone in the restaurant, when all of a sudden, out of nowhere, the figure of a woman will appear. She stares intently at the employee, perhaps overseeing their performance in the beloved restaurant that removed her from a life of night walking. Sometimes, she is not staring at them but rather out the window into the street. Her gaze is intense, seemingly looking for someone long since passed into the afterlife. She is always wearing white, and appears in full form, rather than a ghostly transparency. However, she vanishes before the very eyes of whoever looks upon her.

Poltergeist activity is also reported. Many employees report stacking chairs at the end of the night or setting them out at the beginning of the day and then head into the back room. When they return, they are horrified to see that all of the chairs have been silently moved. There have also been numerous reports of workers in the back room of the restaurant hearing the crashing and moving of chairs and glassware, only to come out to the dining room and find every dish in place, every chair neatly pushed in.

The poltergeist that resides in Annabelle's apparently does not limit their activity to the restaurant. The lobby of the Gilmore, just next door, will often have the paper shredder in the office turn on suddenly, often when a stray hand is near its dangerous mouth. The office has also been the scene of another full apparition, this one of Mr. Gilmore himself. He is seen hard at work at his desk, oblivious to the world around him and appearing as real as you or I. He has also been seen through the windows, nervously pacing back and forth and smoking his cigar, just as he did in his last days, alone and deep in endless thought.

The Hotel itself is alive with paranormal activity. Lights turn on and off by themselves, and a general feeling of uneasiness permeates the space. Often, that uneasiness happens in the stairwell to the second story. One hotel worker felt this uneasy feeling and happened to have a camera with her. She snapped a photograph as a cold, deathly wind ran through her body. Upon developing it she discovered she had captured the ghostly image of a solitary, floating arm in the photo that was most definitely not in the stairwell with her that night. Many guests and workers report that shortly after the uneasy feeling on the stairs, the unmistakable shadow of a man is seen, walking slowly down the stairs with no earthly body attached. But the truly ghostly phenomenon does not occur in the lobby or the restaurant, but in the rooms.

A well respected member of Southeast Alaska's business community who wanted to remain anonymous related a story about her stay in the Gilmore Hotel. It is typical of what is reported to occur well into the witching hour when the town is asleep. She and a colleague were on a yearly Spring trip to Ketchikan. Finished with business for the day and exhausted, they decided to turn in early. To save money they shared a room and soon both had drifted off to sleep. Around 2 a.m., the woman awoke to a general feeling of uneasiness, a feeling that something was not right. Suddenly, her colleague sat up in her bed and in a calm, deeper than usual voice declared that "...the hotel is on fire." She then just as suddenly laid back down and was fast asleep.

Knowing the history of the area around her, the fire scorched story of Bill Mitchell, this woman's sleep did not come quite as quickly. She tossed and turned; playing in her mind the story of the arsonist and the fireproof building she slept in that night. Then, out of nowhere, she felt the presence of another in her room. The presence approached her bedside, soft steps coming closer and sat beside her on her bed. To her horror, she clearly saw a depression form on her bed and felt the weight of a body next to her, though nobody was there. She did not believe in ghosts; she still does not. But needless to say, sleep remained elusive that night.

She is not the only person to have ghostly experiences in the rooms. Several guests have reported waking up in the middle of the night, an uneasy fear and a strange floating sensation coursing through their bodies. When they awaken and wipe the sleep out of their eyes, they come to discover that they are not in their beds, but in fact are floating several feet above their beds! A woman named Nancy, who works at the front desk and lives at the hotel, has woken to find a shadowy apparition peering out her window. She also has had a similar experience as the businesswoman. Late at night, finding herself lying next to an obvious weight of a person, see the depression of on her bed, but no one is there.

The Gilmore Hotel is undoubtedly one of the most haunted structures in Alaska. Independent reports claim similar hauntings. Though a history of crime and tragedy is everywhere around it, what is strange about the Gilmore Hotel is that nothing malicious or sorrowful has been known to occur there. The arson did not affect the building. Lizzie and Pat Gilmore both died of natural causes. Annabelle eventually married and she too died happily of natural causes many years after her restaurant days were over. However, eyewitnesses to the apparitions have, on numerous occasions, positively identified the spirits as all three of these people when shown their photos. Could it be that it is not sadness, but fondness that keeps these spirits bound to the building? Could the memories of love, hard work and success hold a soul as quickly as loss and untimely death? How many spirits haunt this actively haunted hotel? Certainly, though the hotel itself never burned down, many buildings surrounding it did. Was the ghostly, deep voice the businesswoman heard a residual memory from a guest during the rash of fires Bill Mitchell started? Could it be, rather, something left over from the fires that rocked the street earlier in the 1920s? As of right now, these questions are still unanswered, and the spirits are still not talking.

Bibliography

Adams, Joshua. n.d. *The Life and Times of the Alaskan Hotel.* Self Published.

Allen, June. 1995. "Gilmore Name a Part of Ketchikan." *Ketchikan Daily News*, August 21.

—. 2002. *SitNews: Stories in the News, A Man Who Changed the Face of a City: The Firebug Bill Mitchell.* November 15. Accessed 2015. http://www.sitnews.org/JuneAllen/Firebug/111502_bill_mitchell.html.

—. 2004. *SitNews: Stories in the News, Ketchikan's Volunteer Legacy: Buckets to Hydrants to Hi-Tech.* January 15. Accessed 2015. http://www.sitnews.net/JuneAllen/KFD/011504_ktn_fire_dept.html.

Andrews, Clarence Leroy. 1916. "Alaska Under the Russians." *The Washington Historical Quarterly*, July: 202-216.

Barnhardt, Carol. 2001. "A History of Schooling for Alaska Native People." *Journal of American Indian Education* Volume 40, Number 1.

Belanger, Jeff. 2003. *Ghost Village.* September 6. Accessed 2015. http://www.ghostvillage.com/legends/2003/legends26_09062003.shtml.

Black, Lydia. 2004. *Russians in Alaska: 1732-1867.* Fairbanks: University of Alaska Press.

Brady, Jeff. 2013. *Skagway: City of the New Century.* Skagway: Lynn Canal Publishing.

Brennan, Tom. 2005. *Cold Crime: How Police Detectives Solved Alaska's Most Shocking Cases.* Kenmore: Epicenter Press.

Catherine Holder Spude, Karl Gurcke, Gwen Hurst and David Huelsbeck. 2006. *The Mascot Saloon Archaeological Investigations in Skagway, Alaska.* Skagway: National Park Service, US Department of the Interior, Klondike Gold Rush National Histoical Park.

Colp, Harry D. 1997. *The Strangest Story Ever Told.* Exposition Press.

Democrat, St. Louis Globe. 1883. "An Alaskan Ghost Story." *The New York Times* , August 22nd.

Harrington, Louise Brinck. 2007. *SitNews: Stories in the News, Pioneers of Southeast Alaska: Patrick J. Gilmore, Sr.* January 17. Accessed 2015. http://www.sitnews.us/Pioneers/Gilmore/011707_patrick_gilmore.html.

Johnson, Julie. 2003 . *A Wild and Discouraging Mess: The History of the White Pass Unit of the Klondike Gold Rush National Historical Park.* Alaska System Support Office: National Park Service.

Lyon, Robert. 2010. *Jeff. Smith's Parlor Museum Historic Structure Report Klondike Gold Rush National Historical Park.* Skagway: U.S. Department of the Interior, National Park Service, Alaska Regional Office.

Martin, Mary Catharine. 2013. *Capital City Weekly.* October 30. Accessed 2015. http://www.capitalcityweekly.com/stories/103013/ae_1180105353.shtml.

Morrison, Ken Coates and Bill. 1991. *The Sinking of the Princess Sophia: Taking the North Down With Her.* St. Louis: Turtleback Books.

n.d. *National Register of Historic Places Registration Form.* NFS Form 10-900 (Rev. 8-86)OMB No. 10244018 , United States Department of the Interior National Park Service .

Roppel, Patricia. 1999. ""Where Can I Buy One of These?" A History of Ketchikan Alaska's Business Community, Wrangell, AK." *Alaska History: A Publication of the Alaska Historical Society.*

Shaw, Katherine Elizabeth (Messerschmidt). n.d. *Juneau Public Library, Messerschmidt/Shaw.* Accessed 2015. www.juneau.org/library/museum/GCM/readarticle.php?UID=951&newxtkey= .

Simpson, Sherry. 1990. "Juneau." *The Alaska Geographic Society* 18.

Smith, Jeff. 2009. *Alias Soapy Smith: The Life and Death of a Scoundrel.* Klondike Research.

Spude, Robert L. S. 1983. *Skagway-District of Alaska-1884-1912: Building the Gateway to the Klondike.* Anthropology and Historic Preservation, Cooperative Park Studies Unit, University of Alaska.

White, Alan, interview by Ian Punnett. 2011. *Coast to coast AM radio program with guest* (October 29).

About the Author

James P. Devereaux is a writer, archaeologist and adventurer who has spent his life in search of good stories to tell. With his bachelor's degree in anthropology from the University of Illinois Urbana-Champaign, Devereaux first moved to Alaska in 2005 to work as an archaeologist for the U.S. military. Since then, his trail through the north has led to him working as a mountain and river guide, a National Park Service archaeologist, a log cabin carpenter and a news reporter for a local radio station. His last five years in the Last Frontier were spent in Skagway, where he fell in love with the scenery and stories of the Southeast Alaska.

As an avid historian whose job it is to study the lives of the dead, it was only a matter of time before he put his interests and talents together to write about the history of some of the Inside Passage's most well-known ghost stories.

Devereaux moved out of Skagway in 2014 with all his possessions, wife and dog packed into his Ford Ranger and now lives in Prairie du Chien, Wisconsin, where he works for Effigy Mounds National Monument. When he's not working to preserve history, he enjoys casting fishing lures into tree branches on the Mississippi River, drinking good craft beers at bonfires and adventuring in the Driftless Area with his wife, Katie, and dog, Scarlette.

If you have a story about any paranormal phenomena that you would like to see in print, please email the author with your name, contact information, and a description of the event at AlaskaGhosts@gmail.com. Your story could be included in an upcoming publication.

Made in the USA
Lexington, KY
17 February 2017